DRIFTING!

"I'm very ... dizzy," Song-Ye said over the suit radio. "Every direction I look, I feel like I'm falling."

Before Dyl managed to connect his end, she fumbled with the connection of her anchor tether and scrabbled with her gloved hands, trying to catch hold of the station, but she came loose. As she flailed for something to hold onto, she only managed to knock herself farther away, while bumping a thin antenna loose as well. Song-Ye floated off, heading toward one of the big, mirrored panels of the solar-power collectors, while Dyl was still a handsbreadth away from his own anchor point. So close ... and yet he was unable to reach it! He tried to move, but Song-Ye continued to drift outward, and when her tether stretched taut, she yanked him along with her. They were both going to crash into the delicate solar collectors.

"We're loose!" Dyl called into the suit radio. "A little help here?" He flew past Mira, who extended her arm to grab him, but missed.

If they struck the solar array, they would cause great damage, maybe even disrupt power to the station ... and without enough power, the ISSC couldn't run its experiments, its life-support, its communications. But if they *didn't* hit the array, they would go drifting out to ... nowhere!

"The *Star Challengers* adventure stories could help to inspire a whole new generation of young women to value science and seek careers in high-tech, engineering and space exploration. These teenage *Star Challengers* team up in their quest to find innovative solutions to help them solve problems using real out-of-this-world science."

—Dr. Sally Ride,
Astronaut

"In no other regime do reality and fiction seem to meet as commonly as in space. No wonder young (and old) people are inspired and excited when reading the *Star Challengers* series. It would be a great item to take along on one's next interplanetary voyage."

—Norm Augustine,
Retired Chairman and CEO, Lockheed Martin Corporation

"There's a reason why the best science fiction takes place in space. It's the only true frontier left. Kids know this. So too does the *Star Challengers* series. Therein is the magical recipe to ensure a future in space for the rest of us."

—Neil deGrasse Tyson,
Astrophysicist, American Museum of Natural History

"Challenger Center continues to be a champion for the future. Young readers will readily identify with the *Star Challengers* characters. The future needs them, and they will respond—in wonderful ways."

—Barbara Morgan,
NASA's First Educator Astronaut

"Ad astra! To the stars! By the way of good stories! Thank you for *Star Challengers*, Rebecca Moesta and Kevin J. Anderson."

—Clay Morgan,
Author of *The Boy Who Spoke Dog*

"June Scobee Rodgers is a woman on a mission and that mission continues to expand. By nature June is an encourager and an inspiration. She has worked to bring renewed interest in science education and space travel through the *Star Challengers* series which will help feed young, curious minds with the possibilities that await them in the future. I can't recommend these books more. Move over Avatar ... here comes Commander Zota."

—Debbie Macomber,
#1 *New York Times* Bestselling Author

"Space may be the final frontier according to *Star Trek*, but if our message to the next generation is to reach for the stars, then the *Star Challengers* series is a great place to start. Our future survival will depend upon how our young students meet the challenge of combining science, engineering, mathematics & imagination."

—Lee Greenwood,
Entertainer, Writer, Musician, Singer & Council Member
for the National Endowment for the Arts

"What if Earth's future rested on the shoulders of five ordinary teens living in present times? And what if a visitor from the future accompanies them through time and space for the adventure of their lives? I was charmed by the premise of *Star Challengers*, a new and innovative series geared to teen readers especially drawn to science and space technology. Never a dull moment in these fast paced books with a winsome cast of inventive kids whose ideas and solutions help make a difference for our planet. Every reader can relate to their cause and challenges. All readers will be caught up in their all too human relationships with one another and humankind from tomorrow. I found the stories infused with nail biting adventure, romance and plausible science. Skip the vampires! Don't miss this thought-provoking series presented by June Scobee Rodgers and the Challenger Center for Space Science Education and written by award-winning, international bestselling authors Rebecca Moesta & Kevin J. Anderson."

—Lurlene McDaniel,
Bestselling Young-Adult Author

Praise for the Challenger Centers for Space Science Education

"Inspiring. Exploring. Learning. It's our mission. That's hard to beat!"

—John Glenn,
Former Senator and Astronaut

"The mission of Challenger Center is to spark in our young people an interest—and a joy—in science. A spark that can change their lives—and help make American enterprise the envy of the world."

—Former President George H. W. Bush

"What Challenger Center has done with respect to educating America's youth is truly commendable. I salute you."

—General Colin Powell,
Former Secretary of State

"Challenger Center is at the forefront of space science education for elementary and middle school students ... America's leaders and explorers of tomorrow."

—Michael L. Coats,
Director, NASA Johnson Space Center

"[Students] will see something and experience something that they perhaps read about, but could not truly appreciate until they came and experienced it."

—Frederick Gregory,
NASA Associate Administrator and Former Astronaut

June Scobee Rodgers Presents:

STAR CHALLENGERS #2
Space Station Crisis

Rebecca Moesta & Kevin J. Anderson

STAR CHALLENGERS: SPACE STATION CRISIS

Cover Art by John E. Kaufmann • Art Direction by Brent Evans
Copy Edited by John Helfers • Layout and Logo Design by Matt Heerdt
Production by Randall N. Bills • Licensing by Loren L. Coleman

Published by Catalyst Game Labs, an imprint of InMediaRes Productions, LLC
PMB 202 • 303 91st Ave NE • E502 • Lake Stevens, WA 98258
ISBN: 978-1-934857-66-3

First Edition: January 2011 • Printed in the USA

www.challenger.org
(Challenger Centers For Space Science Education)
www.wordfire.com
(Explore the Universes of Kevin J. Anderson & Rebecca Moesta)
www.StarChallengers.com
(Star Challengers)
www.CatalystGameLabs.com
(Catalyst Game Labs' web pages)
www.battlecorps.com/catalog
(online ordering)

DEDICATION

To the Challenger Center flight directors, teachers,
and astronauts everywhere who help launch young people
toward discovery and achievement.

ACKNOWLEDGMENTS

We are grateful to the countless people who have given their support to the Star Challengers project. In particular, we would like to thank:

Pam Peterson, Dan Barstow, and Bill Readdy of the Challenger Centers for Space Science Education; Loren Coleman, Randall Bills, and Brent Evans at Catalyst Game Labs; John Silbersack at Trident Media Group; Diane Jones and Louis Moesta at WordFire, Inc.; Mary Thomsen for her twinkle-fingered transcriptions and useful additions; Cherie Buchheim and first-reader Debra Ray for their lifelong-space-geek insights; Alan & Rebecca Lickiss and Sarah & Dan Hoyt for their problem-solving assistance years ago when this project was in its infancy; Rose and Bill Narva; Don Rodgers for cheering us on; Louise Moesta, Jonathan & Jessica Cowan, Tim Jones, and Sarah & Joe Thompson for smoothing the road, so Kevin & Rebecca could stay on track; June's grandchildren who encouraged and offered their suggestions; Kevin & Rebecca's grandson for giving us a glimpse of the generation to come; space artist Bob McCall (deceased) and astronaut entrepreneur Richard Garriott, who helped create the Challenger Center design; Allen Steele for recognizing that June, Rebecca, and Kevin absolutely had to work together; the CLC flight directors and teachers around the world who inspire students to aim for the stars; Susan Weikel Morrison; Dr. Harry Kloor; our technical advisers and brainstormers astronaut/MD Scott Parazynski, Colonel Richard Scobee, and Dr. Edward B. Tomme.

ONE

The sky was calling JJ.

She needed to get her feet off the ground and be surrounded by nothing but air—while going very, very fast. With razor focus, she worked her way through the preflight checklist while standing next to the compact Piper Arrow. All the while, her uncle Buzz watched her like a hawk.

"Take your time," he cautioned. "The sky's not going anywhere." He'd been her flight instructor long enough that JJ knew if she didn't do a good job following the checklist, she wouldn't be going anywhere either.

When she finished the checklist, forcing herself to pay attention to every detail, he smiled and said, "Good job, flygirl. Got your pubs bag?" She nodded and held up the small heavy bag that held her approach plates, charts, and logbook. "Then let's see how you do getting this baby off the ground."

JJ—short for "Jenny June"—Wren climbed into the Arrow's cockpit, feeling a little bit nervous and a whole lot excited. Today would be her first time piloting a plane in weather under IFR—instrument flight rules. She'd have to trust her instruments when she couldn't see where she was flying. Uncle Buzz had chosen an overcast day specifically so that she could practice using her instruments. It was an entirely different experience.

Up until now, she had been learning on her uncle's crop duster, which had an open cockpit. But she could only fly the crop duster under visual flight rules, keeping her eyes open and watching where she was going. This would be a big step for her. Though she had flown in the single-engine Piper a few times, this was her first time as the actual pilot. The responsibility and the freedom were thrilling.

Uncle Buzz folded his tall frame into the copilot's seat to her right. JJ casually tossed the pubs bag onto the back seat, buckled herself in, and put on her headset. When Uncle Buzz gave her the thumbs-up sign, she signaled the tower. "Tower, this is Arrow November nine zero five zero kilo, ready for takeoff, runway one-seven right, IFR round-robin." She tried to sound serious, professional, and older than her actual fourteen years. Uncle Buzz had taught her the code, how to talk like a real pilot.

Air Traffic Control, or ATC, responded, "Arrow November nine zero five zero kilo, you are cleared for take-off. Fly heading one-eight-zero, climb to twenty-five hundred, and contact departure." That vector would take them around the approaching storm. JJ wasn't worried (if anything, Uncle Buzz thought she didn't worry enough). Biting her lower lip in concentration, she lined up the small plane on the runway, confirming with the compass that it matched the runway heading, then gradually pushed up the throttle.

"Okay, now that we're moving," her uncle said, "how's your engine?"

JJ checked the gauges. "Pressure green, temperature green." She loved feeling the thrum of the plane as she accelerated down the runway. "Airspeed alive," she said when the indicator started showing her speed.

Uncle Buzz gave her another thumbs-up. When they were going fast enough, JJ slowly pulled back on the yoke—the control that looked a little like a steering wheel. With just a slight wobble, the Arrow's wheels lifted off the ground. JJ's heart seemed to lift off at the same time as the lightweight plane. As the little craft climbed toward the clouds on the heading that ATC had given her, JJ reminded herself of all of the times she had practiced this in a simulator.

Now it was real.

"Bring your nose down just a little, for your best angle of climb," Uncle Buzz said.

JJ did, and she had just started feeling relaxed—even giddy—when a gust hit the plane, but she adjusted easily and flew through the mild turbulence. She could handle this. The Arrow hit more rough air when they reached the clouds, but again JJ held the aircraft steady on its heading. She liked this! JJ imagined she was having a little competition with the weather, and she was determined to win.

Piloting this plane reminded her of the Challenger Center simulations—which had turned out to be quite real. She couldn't just learn things halfway. She *was* going to be a pilot, and a good one. The mysterious Commander Zota had convinced JJ and her friends that lives would depend on them in the future.

She was reveling in the flight when a downdraft slammed them like a giant invisible flyswatter. For a few seconds, it felt as if the plane dropped out from beneath her like one of those long-plunge freefall rides at an amusement park, and her stomach tried to float up into her throat. But she didn't panic; she knew what to do. JJ sucked in a deep breath to steady herself and concentrated on flying even as turbulence shook the aircraft.

Another strong gust smacked them, then—*wham!*— something hard struck JJ on the back of the head, and everything went gray and fuzzy…

The next thing she knew, an acrid chemical smell was filling her nostrils, and everything came into clear focus with a jolt. From the copilot's seat, Uncle Buzz waved something that looked like a roll of gauze under her nose—the source of the horrible smell. Her eyes and nose stung, but she was fully awake.

"What…?" JJ began.

"Good, that snapped you out of it. Took me a couple minutes to get us into clear airspace, but we're fine now." Uncle Buzz threw the small tube of gauze into the back seat. "Smelling salts—very useful in an emergency like that. Most pilots don't carry them, but I'm old fashioned about my first aid kit. You were looking a bit woozy there. It tends to happen when you get banged on the head."

JJ put a hand to the back of her skull, which was throbbing. "Wha—how?" she asked, then remembered to put both hands back on the yoke. She tightened her grip. "Who hit me?"

"There was an embedded thunderstorm in the clouds. After ATC gave us our heading, the storm must've moved faster than expected. We caught the edge of it, and the winds knocked us around a bit. And when we hit that downdraft, the pubs bag came up out of the back seat and whacked you on the noggin. Next time, remember to stow it and strap it down."

JJ felt herself flush with embarrassment at the stupid mistake. "Sorry, I won't forget next time, and I certainly won't forget that smell!" She wrinkled her nose in disgust. "It sure cleared my head fast."

"Ammonia salts," Uncle Buzz explained. "You weren't unconscious, but it wouldn't hurt to let a doctor look at that head once we land. How are you doing?"

"Other than feeling like an idiot, you mean? Fine." JJ was determined to get things right, and she would not make that particular mistake again. "I'd like to do the landing, if that's all right," she said. "Someone has to take us back down—and it might as well be me."

Uncle Buzz gave her a thumbs-up again. "But you let me know if you feel dizzy."

Clouds and the speckles of mist on the cockpit windshield made it impossible to see, but she followed her instruments. IFR. *That* was her challenge for today. She contacted the tower again, and Air Traffic Control provided a return heading. Using the numbers and the compass, she turned the plane back toward the small runway.

She watched the altimeter as she descended, pretending not to notice that Uncle Buzz kept a sharp eye on the instruments as well. Fortunately, he didn't need to correct her. Though her head still throbbed, JJ knew she was following procedures to the letter. The instruments told her she was on the correct flight path.

Suddenly, like a curtain being yanked away from a window, the haze of moisture disappeared as the Piper Arrow dropped below the gray clouds. The rolling landscape spread out before her, and in the distance she saw the airport with its small control tower. Far to her left, she spotted another small plane just climbing to the clouds. Otherwise the sky was empty. What a relief to see where she was going again!

Over the radio she heard, "Arrow November nine zero five zero kilo, report runway in sight."

"Arrow November nine zero five zero kilo—runway in sight," she said.

"Arrow November nine zero five zero kilo, cleared to land, runway one-seven right."

She tensed briefly, forced herself to relax, then glanced at the instruments. She could tell Uncle Buzz was proud of her. Her father, a firefighter killed in the line of duty two years ago, would have been proud, too. The runway drew her toward it like a magnet, and she aligned the Arrow perfectly.

The plane felt natural gliding down toward the pavement. The wheels touched down with just a bump, and then they were roaring along the ground, decelerating like a drag racer. She felt an adrenaline rush as she slowed the Piper to a safe ground speed and brought them to their designated spot.

Laughing, Uncle Buzz gave her a one-man round of applause.

JJ couldn't have been more pleased. "I need this practice if I'm going to be a pilot someday," she said. In her mind, however, she was thinking, *a spaceship pilot*.

These lessons were a thrill, but they had a serious purpose. Thanks to their recent Challenger Center adventure, JJ and her friends knew something that Uncle Buzz did not: An alien invasion was coming in the not-too-distant future, and Earth had only a generation to prepare for it. The skills they learned now might some-day mean the difference between life and death for the human race.

TWO

Dylan pushed speed-dial 4 on his cell phone; he'd been using that number a lot in the past month. Ever since their amazing trip to Moonbase Magellan and escaping from the Kylarn attack, one of them had called or emailed the other almost every day, just to check in.

Song-Ye picked up on the second ring and spoke immediately, having seen his name on the caller ID. She didn't bother with any of the polite pleasantries that usually started a phone conversation. "You'll never guess where I am, Junior."

Donovan Dylan Wren, Dyl for short, no longer minded that the South Korean girl kept calling him *Junior*. The nickname had become a friendly joke between them, and they were learning to appreciate each other's sense of humor. "Hmm … are you exploring a ship-wreck in the Caribbean?" he teased.

Using his shoulder to press the phone against his ear, Dyl stirred a pot of spaghetti sauce with a long wooden spoon. He sat in front of the stove on a rolling stool he used when cooking for the family. He didn't need his crutches in the kitchen. On the floor, their tuxedo cat Spock rubbed against his ankles.

"That's your best guess—the Caribbean? As in, swimming with sharks? No, thank you," Song-Ye said. "Try again, Junior."

Dyl tasted the sauce and added some oregano. "Are you at the Rose Bowl, watching a football game?"

Song-Ye made her usual *pfft* sound that meant she was dismissing his comment. "I'm not a football fan. I really don't understand why people want to watch a bunch of guys in fat-suits chasing a big brown egg up and down a field. One more guess."

Dyl tried to be as outlandish as possible. "Buckingham Palace, then?"

"Ooh—close! Actually, I'm at a diplomatic reception at the British Embassy with my father."

"Because...?" He knew her father was a diplomat, and Song-Ye often found herself in VIP situations that neither Dyl nor his sister JJ ever encountered.

"Because he didn't want to go alone, and Mom was called away for an emergency consult at Johns Hopkins Hospital—something about a Prime Minister with heart problems."

"I thought you hated stuff like fancy receptions." He tried to sound as if he was commiserating, but didn't think he pulled it off.

Dyl could almost hear her shrugging one shoulder as she replied, "Normally, I do. These events can be kind of tedious. But Commander Zota wanted us to broaden our horizons and learn new things. There's a lot at stake. In fact, I'm actually wearing a cocktail dress."

"An alien-fighting cocktail dress?" He wasn't sure how dressing up for a diplomatic party would help prepare them for the arrival of the Kylarn.

"A professional-looking cocktail dress, appropriate for meeting all sorts of world-class leaders. It's midnight blue with tiny crystals sewn across it so that it looks like a starry night."

"Now *that* I'd like to see—uh, purely for scientific purposes, of course. Maybe I could identify some of the constellations. I've been studying a little astronomy, you know, to do my part…."

She laughed. He liked it when she laughed. Dyl realized he was blushing. He could hear a muffled chatter of voices in the background, a piano playing. "Uh, aren't you supposed to be keeping your father from getting bored right now?"

"Not really. He's talking to the Duke of Something-or-Other. They were in the same college at Oxford—Merton, I think. Besides, it's a cocktail reception, and I'm the only person here not drinking—for obvious reasons. So I stepped out on the patio for a few minutes." She paused, then lowered her voice. "Are you getting excited yet?"

"About a diplomatic reception?" Dyl misunderstood her on purpose.

"*Junior*," she said in mock exasperation.

"Oh, you mean about going back to the Challenger Center this weekend? Of course I am. I've been working on the assignment Mr. Zota gave us. I even figured out a way to get extra credit at school." The enigmatic commander had promised that if they spent the month learning three new things according to his instructions, he would send them on another mission—into the future. And so Dyl, JJ, Song-Ye, and their friend Elton Elijah King had all been busy "earning" their next adventure.

Dyl put a pot of water on the stove for boiling the spaghetti noodles. Their mother would be home from her waitressing job any minute now, and it was Dyl's turn to fix dinner. Later, while Mrs. Wren got ready to go to her evening job at the hotel, JJ would clean the kitchen. For now, his sister was doing homework in the living room.

On the phone, Song-Ye said, "Only two more days."

"Check. T-minus two days and counting—over." He turned on the timer for the pasta.

"Whatever. See you there, Junior. Over and out."

JJ sat by the coffee table on the living room floor, doing her algebra problems and enjoying the aromas of baking garlic bread and simmering spaghetti sauce. The entire apartment smelled like an Italian restaurant. She also enjoyed the fact that Tony Vasquez sat next to her. Sure, he was here getting help on math, but his well-to-do parents could have afforded a private tutor, if he'd wanted one. Instead, he chose to be here with JJ.

Tony ran a hand through his curly light-brown hair and sighed. "I don't know why I'm so dense. I ought to know this stuff. Boy, you'd think my parents were crash-test dummies instead of computer scientists."

JJ snorted. "You're not dumb. This not-getting-algebra is just temporary. You're great at lots of subjects, this one's just taking a little longer."

He looked sidelong at her, and the worry in his blue-green eyes faded. "And how do you know I'm not an idiot?"

Looking up at the ceiling, JJ pursed her lips and thought for a moment. Her blond ponytail swished and tickled the back of her neck. "Well, you always solve mysteries halfway through the movie, you can do Sudoku puzzles in a flash. You made it to Level 100 of *Rampart Raids IV* faster than anyone I know, plus you built a robot that took first place at the science fair last year. Besides, I predict that you're going to learn this *soon*, because you have a good tutor."

He laughed at that. "Sure, she's modest, too. Anyway, what if I'm just faking being bad at algebra so I can spend time with you?"

JJ could feel her face getting pink. "Well, in that case, I like the way you think."

"Do you have time to tutor me on Saturday?"

She shook her head, hating to turn him down. "I've got kind of a ... *thing* on Saturday." And there was no way she would miss it.

He raised his eyebrows. "A *thing*?"

"An exercise, I'd guess you'd say," JJ said evasively. She wasn't supposed to talk about how the Star Challengers had gone to the future, visited the Moon, and tried to save Moonbase Magellan. Not that Tony would believe her anyway. "It's at the Challenger Center."

"Hey, that was my favorite field trip ever! Made me think of how awesome it would be to be a real astronaut. That simulation was very realistic."

JJ was surprised by his enthusiasm. *And you don't know the half of it*, she thought.

"Believe me, sometimes when I'm doing routines on the rings or parallel bars, I think about what it would feel like to be totally weightless."

Tony was one of the top gymnasts at their high school. Sometimes JJ stayed after school to watch him practice. Tony could do an iron cross on the rings, which showed how strong his arms and shoulders were. It had always amazed her that someone so smart was also so athletic.

"I'm going to be an astronaut," JJ said. "That's one reason I love going to the Challenger Center."

"So, what's the program? Can I come along?" He glanced down at the algebra book, but pushed the homework aside. "I just happen to be free on Saturday."

"I..." JJ felt awkward. Commander Zota had chosen their team specifically, briefed them on the realities of living in space and on the Moon, and sent them on their mission. That adventure had convinced the Star Challengers how urgent it was for the next generation to learn about science, math, and engineering. Zota had also given them a stern warning not to reveal the truth of who he was and what he could do.

"Well, I'd love to have you there, but ... it's sort of a private deal—my brother and me, and a couple of others." Spock sauntered in from the kitchen, jumped onto the coffee table, and purred loudly for attention. JJ petted him, not sure what else to tell her friend. "Maybe another time."

Tony looked disappointed, but he forced a smile. "I remember you saying you would go to the Moon someday. 'Moon, sweet Moon,' right? Of all the people who talk about things like that, I actually believe you could do it."

For a moment, JJ saw it all again in her mind—the stark beauty of the lunar surface, how she could jump high off the ground with so little effort (even in her bulky space suit), the meteor showers ... the alien attacks. She sighed. "Yeah. Moon, sweet Moon."

Tony propped his elbow on the coffee table and put his chin on his hand. "Well, if you're going to be an astronaut, maybe I'll become a rocket scientist."

JJ thought about the quest that Zota had given them—to encourage people their age to study sciences. The human race needed more scientists. Maybe she could convince him to let Tony go on a future mission.

She brightened. "Know what rocket scientists have to learn?"

"What?"

"*Math.*" She nudged Spock off of the algebra book and pushed it back toward Tony.

He pounded his fist against his palm, like a fighter getting ready to take on an opponent. "Then let's focus on the homework and get this done."

THREE

JJ's heart raced at the sight of the Challenger Center when their mom drove up to drop her and Dyl off. Her brother fidgeted with anticipation of the day's upcoming adventure. The Center was still the same squat, unassuming brick building it had always been, with a large-scale model of a rocket standing tall in front of it. But now that JJ and Dyl knew what was inside, it seemed more tantalizing.

"I'm glad you're excited about this," said Mrs. Wren, "especially since I have to pull an extra shift today. You enjoyed Mr. Zota's last simulation so much that I know you'll have a good time. Are you sure I don't need to pick you up?"

"Already got it covered," JJ assured her.

"Song-Ye's driver Winston will take us home afterward—in a *limo*," Dyl said. "Cool, huh?"

JJ added, "We've made some good friends."

Climbing out of the car, Dyl set his crutches firmly on the pavement and moved aside. Although he would never walk normally, he had adapted well since the car accident that had injured him.

Mrs. Wren said, "Love you both whole bunches."

"Love you, Mom," JJ and Dyl replied in unison.

JJ closed both of the car doors while Dyl pretended to speak into an imaginary voice recorder. "Cadet's Log, T-minus 5 minutes and counting. We are on final approach to the space center." He gave JJ a mock salute and swung forward on his crutches, heading toward the Challenger Center building.

JJ could see they weren't the only ones excited about the meeting. King and Song-Ye were already waiting outside the door, having arrived separately. Petite and graceful, Song-Ye had straight black hair and dark eyes that seemed to mock the world. King, who was six feet tall, had light brown skin, a mellow voice, and a confident manner.

They all exchanged greetings and hugs and spent the next few minutes in animated chatter. The friends agreed that emails, texts, and phone calls were no substitute for being together.

JJ turned in surprise when a dark blue Lexus sedan drove up and pulled to the curb in front of the Challenger Center.

"Are we expecting anyone else?" King asked.

JJ opened her mouth to answer, but no words came out, as the car door opened and a grinning Tony Vasquez emerged. He saw JJ and waved.

Tony's father leaned over and called, "Have a good time. Give it your best, Antonio."

"Believe me, I will, Dad." Tony shut the car door and bounded with a gymnast's grace up the sidewalk as the Lexus drove away. "Bet you didn't think I was coming!" he said to JJ.

"Looks like *somebody* blabbed," Dyl whispered.

JJ finally managed to speak. "Tony ... what are you doing here? I said–"

"I told you, I really enjoyed that Challenger Center field trip. So I'm going to ask if I can participate. There's always room for one more, right? What's the worst they can say?" While a flustered JJ tried to think of a response, he turned to Song-Ye and King. "Hi, I'm Tony Vasquez. I go to school with JJ and Dylan."

King shook his hand. Song-Ye gave him a skeptical look. "Whatever."

The building door opened, and a trim man with dusky skin and a jagged scar down his left cheek nodded in welcome. In spite of his pure white hair, Commander Zota did not look the least bit old. "Greetings, Cadets." Consternation filled the flight director's gray eyes when he caught sight of Tony. "And who might our guest be?"

JJ, secretly glad to see Tony, knew she was responsible for explaining his presence. "This is my friend Tony from school, and this is Commander Zota. Tony and I were doing homework together, and I might have mentioned something about today. He was so impressed with our class field trip to the Challenger Center that he just … showed up."

Tony reached out and shook Zota's hand. "Nice to meet you, sir. I saw you when our class came here for a mission last month. I'd like to join the group, if you'll let me. I promise I'll take the assignment seriously, whatever you give me."

The commander gestured them inside, still acting somewhat cool. "Indeed, we may have to make a few … adjustments to accommodate a new crewmember. Would you be so kind, Cadet Vasquez, as to wait while Cadet Wren"— he glanced pointedly at JJ—"assists me briefly."

Tony took a seat on the bench just inside the doorway, against the corridor wall. Dyl and King sat beside him. Song-Ye made a beeline for a colorful plastic rodent habitat at the back of the round lobby. "Newton!" She took the hamster out and held him gently in one hand while stroking his head with the other. They had rescued the hamster from Moonbase Magellan in the future, just before the base was attacked.

JJ followed Commander Zota down the hallway and into the small briefing room. Under other circumstances, JJ loved this room. The ceiling twinkled with fiber-optic stars on a field of black, and a round light representing the Sun shone from the center of a model of the solar system overhead. At the moment, however, JJ suspected she was about to receive a stern lecture.

"Mr. Vasquez did not receive an invitation," Commander Zota began. "Remember, I selected you four *specifically*. We have so much to do, and it could be quite dangerous if others learned about our work. I cannot afford to risk the future for just anyone who happens to arrive."

JJ stood up for her friend. "Tony's not just anyone. He's really smart, and I trust him. I'm sorry I mentioned our group, but I didn't invite him. He decided to come *on his own*. It may be impulsive, but it's also pretty brave. Besides, you said one of the reasons you came back in time was to help us get our whole generation interested in science. Tony's interested. Shouldn't we encourage that?"

The commander frowned. "Perhaps, but you must all agree to keep my presence here as secret as possible. That information is on a need-to-know basis, just as your travels in time must be kept quiet. You know how much is at stake. Security cannot be taken lightly. We have enemies out there, and they do not all look like Kylarn."

JJ wasn't entirely convinced that it mattered who knew about Mr. Zota. Even if the truth leaked out, who would believe in time travelers and alien invasions? Still, he was worried. "Got it. I promise to keep it secret from now on, and I'll be sure to remind the others so they understand how serious the situation is. But will you please give Tony a chance? He'd make a great member of the team, and I think he's already leaning toward science as a career."

Zota's face was grave. "Very well. But I remind you, saying anything to anyone about time travel or my role here could have serious consequences."

When they were all in the small briefing room, Zota stood before them in his blue jumpsuit, hands clasped behind his back. "And now, cadets, tell me how you did on your TNT assignments—Three New Things you learned since last we met. Since we have a newcomer, I'll explain what my expectations were."

His gray eyes narrowed as he turned to Tony. "The first part of the TNT challenge was to study at least one new topic related to engineering, mathematics, science, or technology. With these tools, you will build the foundation of your future.

"Part two was to step out of your current routine and learn something that makes you uncomfortable, perhaps something you have been avoiding. Push yourself beyond your comfort zone. This allows you to approach problems from different angles, and helps you to mature.

"Part three was to strengthen your bodies in some new way. The future will make physical, as well as mental, demands of you. And in general, the healthier you are, the easier it is to think clearly. Please begin, Cadet King."

King stopped humming "Eye of the Tiger" and launched into his report. "For the first part, I took a simple intro to electronics course on the Internet. Second, languages aren't really my thing, but I learned how to count and say hello in Russian, Chinese, and French. For physical training, I started kickboxing using a DVD my dad got me. And even though I know it wasn't part of the assignment, I finished my Eagle project, too." He grinned and brushed self-consciously at his shirt. "You are now looking at an official Eagle Scout." His friends clapped and cheered.

"Excellent," Zota said. "Cadet Park?"

From the corner of her eye, JJ saw her brother pull out a stack of notecards and a pencil. He scribbled notes to himself, a habit that helped him do well in school.

"I take ballet lessons, of course," Song-Ye said, "but since we had to do something new, I took a class in hap-ki-do, a Korean form of martial arts." She looked over at Dyl. "And make sure you spell it right, Junior."

"I know how to spell *it*," Dyl quipped.

Song-Ye rolled her eyes. "Other than that, I took a first-aid course, and I read some articles about understanding different cultures." She shrugged one shoulder.

"Dad always wanted me to learn that kind of stuff, even though I didn't want to. It wasn't that bad. I even went to a diplomatic reception with him when my mom was out of town."

Dyl muttered, "I still want to see that dress you wore."

JJ gave Song-Ye an encouraging thumbs-up. Song-Ye raised her eyebrows at JJ. "Did you know that in some countries, the thumbs-up sign is actually considered rude?"

"Cool!" Dyl gave her a teasing thumbs-up. "Just warn me before I go to any of those countries. My turn now? I've been working out every day after school with my friend George—his grandparents live in our building, and they're the ones who tutored me after I got smashed up by that car accident. Anyway, we're lifting weights and doing special exercises for my legs. Even though the doctors don't think I can, I'm hoping to walk without crutches someday. My arms are getting a lot stronger, too."

He pretended to make a muscle-man bicep, and Song-Ye said, "*Pfft*."

Dyl ignored her. "I did some research on physiology, especially the effects of gravity on humans. The hardest thing I did was join the debate team at school to help me get over my fear of speaking in front of people."

"A good choice. And what about our other Cadet Wren?" Zota looked at JJ, who immediately launched into her report.

"Figured I needed to be more versatile, so I started learning to fly a new type of plane, a lot more advanced than a crop duster—that part was awesome, of course.

Also learned to fly under Instrument Flight Rules, instead of just by sight." Zota nodded, as if he had expected this from her. "For the science part, I borrowed a chemistry set from the Sutros down the hall and did some simple experiments. I also found some free Pilates lessons on the Web, so I've been tightening up my core muscles."

"And Cadet Vasquez," Commander Zota said. "Anything to add?"

Tony looked surprised. He ran both hands through his hair and took a deep breath. "Boy, I didn't actually know about the assignment before I got here, but let's see. JJ's been tutoring me in algebra, and I got a B– on our last test. Believe me, that's a big improvement. I learned to do flares on the pommel horse—gymnastics, that is—and I started a private driver's training course. Is that good enough?"

"It is indeed." Mr. Zota looked satisfied. "Now it's time for us to prep for the mission."

FOUR

Now that they had finished their reports, JJ was anxious for the mission to start. About time! Where would Commander Zota send them next?

She whispered out of the side of her mouth to Tony, "You're going to love this."

Although their previous adventure at Moonbase Magellan had been nerve-wracking—not to mention the fact that they had barely escaped with their lives—it was also one of the most intense and significant experiences of her life. JJ and her companions had learned just how important their roles would be in the future.

Tony seemed amused that they were all so wound up about a space simulation. She gave him a secretive smile. He had *no idea* what he had gotten himself into.

"Shall we begin? We have limited time." Commander Zota drew his strangely distant gaze across all of them. "In more ways than one."

Dylan scribbled more notes on his index cards. Watching her brother, JJ saw real excitement, an eager anticipation for their activity, and she remembered how easily he had been able to move in the low gravity on the Moon. For his sake, she hoped they would be sent into a lower gravity environment again, where he could ditch his crutches and get around as well as anyone else.

Song-Ye still cradled her hamster, who seemed happy to cuddle in the crook of her arm. "Can I take Newton along this time, Commander?"

Zota raised an eyebrow, which stretched the scar on his cheek. "No telling what you might encounter on this mission into the future. I think he'll remain safer here."

The Korean girl sighed and nodded. "You're right." She reluctantly returned the furry animal to his habitat.

Tony hid a smile, thinking he was playing along with some kind of script, but JJ knew that Commander Zota was serious.

"Your mission today will be to the International Space Station Complex, or ISSC," Zota explained. On the display board, he showed them a diagram of numerous cylinders linked together in a hodgepodge grid. The modules, connected to each other with smaller hubs, were reinforced with support struts and adorned with long rectangular solar panels that gathered the sun's energy like giant reflective windmills. JJ had seen similar images of the current International Space Station, but this future complex was far more extensive.

Dyl flipped to a new notecard and scribbled a quick sketch with his pencil. "It looks like a bunch of soda cans strung together with Tinker Toys."

"High-tech soda cans," King pointed out.

"The space-station complex is functional enough," Zota said. "It expanded piece by piece over the years, using the current International Space Station as its foundation. In early science fiction stories, designers imagined space stations as graceful rotating wheels in space. But the ISSC had to be built module by module, each component lifted up to orbit and assembled by astronauts."

"At your suggestion, sir, I looked up some of the background on early space stations," King said. "The US built Skylab in 1973, but they abandoned it after only two years, and it burned up on re-entry in 1979. The Russians built the Mir station next, and then in 1998 construction began on the International Space Station." He nodded to the diagram. "But the current ISS is just a tiny outpost compared to this schematic. It sure has grown."

Zota nodded. "In addition to proving that humans can live in space for extended periods, there are many advantages to an orbital facility operating in zero-gravity—or as it is more precisely called, microgravity. The occupants are still very much under the influence of Earth's gravity, even though they don't feel it.

"Science in microgravity is a powerful tool. Gravity is a fundamental physical constant in our world, and going into space allows scientists—those who study biology, chemistry, materials science, combustion physics, and many other disciplines—a rare opportunity to look at their areas of expertise from a completely new vantage point, without the constant pull of gravity. Growing cancer cells in three dimensions in space, as opposed to just a few layers thick in a Petrie dish, is one example of how scientists can use microgravity to their advantage. Many common processes are different in weightlessness: growing crystals, or making pharmaceuticals, exotic materials, and high-density computer chips." He looked at them all, and his gaze lingered longest on Tony. "However, many people have difficulty adapting to the environment. It affects balance, resulting in disorientation."

Dyl grinned. "You say that like it's a bad thing."

"It can indeed be problematic," the commander said.

"I can't wait," Song-Ye said with a distinct lack of enthusiasm.

Dyl pointed out, "We adapted just fine to low gravity on the Moonbase mission."

"*Low* gravity is very different from *no* gravity," Zota said. "I'd like you to participate in an experiment before I send you up there. Come with me."

"Boy, you guys are good at this role-playing stuff," Tony whispered to JJ. "You all talk like you've actually been on the Moon."

Zota led them to the medical station inside the simulator chamber, where he showed them a padded chair that spun smoothly on a highly lubricated axis. "This is a Barany chair. We use it to demonstrate how your body interprets information about equilibrium."

"I saw this during our field trip here from school," Tony said, "but it wasn't my station, and I never got a turn."

"You'll all have a chance before we proceed with transport to orbit," Zota said. "Tell me, what information do you normally use to keep your balance?"

"Sight," Song-Ye said.

"Right. I like to depend on what I see," JJ said. "That's what made flying under IFR so tricky at first."

King grinned. "Usually, I don't have a problem staying balanced if my feet are on the ground. So I guess I'm partly using a sense of touch—the pressure under my feet."

"There's hearing, too," Tony said. "My aunt is blind, but she can tell a lot about where people and things are, just by listening."

"Indeed. Anything else?" Commander Zota asked.

"Piece of cake," Dyl said. "I read about this. There are tiny hairs in your inner ear that tell the brain which way is which. If that gets messed up—like when a person gets an ear infection—it can make you dizzy."

"Excellent." Zota turned to JJ. "Cadet Wren, would you like to be the first test subject?"

"I'm in!" JJ plopped herself into the chair, which had a five-point pilot's harness. She buckled the harness across her waist, between her legs, and over her shoulders and chest. "Now what?"

"For this experiment, we limit the information that your brain normally receives." From the counter Zota lifted earphones and a set of large goggles with a completely opaque lens plate. He slipped the goggles over JJ's head, covering her eyes; the padding fit snugly around her eyes and cheeks. Although her eyes were open, the goggles blocked all light.

For a moment, JJ felt disoriented by a blackness as deep as space, although fortunately she still felt the solid chair beneath her. She tried to imagine herself floating there, like Alexei Leonov, the Soviet Cosmonaut who had been the first human to walk in space in 1965.

"Point your thumbs toward the ceiling, Cadet Wren, and after I spin the chair point your thumbs in the direction you feel you are rotating. When you think you have stopped, point your thumbs straight up again. Simple enough?" The commander's voice seemed to come from nowhere. Everything was so completely dark.

"Simple enough. Spin me." She pressed her back against the chair, ready to go.

"One final step." He placed the snug and heavy headphones on her, and all sound stopped.

And then JJ was whirling around like a ride at a carnival, spinning and spinning. She tilted her thumbs to point in the direction she was circling. It was an amazing illusion. No sight, no sound. To get into the spirit, she thought of herself in a space capsule, rotating around and around…like John Glenn in 1962, the first American to orbit the Earth.

She wondered what was happening in the room around her. King was probably humming "Dizzy" or some other old song. She felt herself stop spinning and gradually start turning the opposite way, so she pointed her thumbs to show the other direction. Commander Zota tugged off the goggles and headphones, and JJ was astonished to find that she was sitting completely still. The feeling was even more disorienting than the silent darkness had been.

"When did I stop?" she asked.

"The chair stopped fifteen seconds ago," Tony said. "Did you really think you were still moving?"

JJ unbuckled the harness and stood up, wobbled a bit, then turned to Tony. "If it's so easy, then you try it." She handed him the goggles. He put them on, set the headphones in place, and sat in the chair. For his turn, she watched Tony spin round and round; he had a grin on his face, enjoying the ride, but he made the same error

JJ had made. Because the chair was perfectly balanced, and he had no visual reference points, he couldn't tell when he stopped spinning.

Dyl went next, then King, both with similar results.

Seeing them all frustrated, Zota explained, "Your confusion came from the fact that the small hairs in your inner ear initially told your brain that you were spinning. After a short time, the fluid in your inner ear began to spin at the same rate as the hairs, so you felt like you had stopped. Finally, the hairs sensed that you were slowing down, but since you thought you were already stopped—without sight or hearing to help you correctly decipher the inner-ear signals—you misinterpreted the slowing down as a reversal to spin in the opposite direction. Now, Cadet Park, if you would be so kind as to sit in the Barany chair…?"

Song-Ye, who had watched everyone else take their turns, hesitated. "I…get dizzy, and I don't like carnival rides."

"Come on, it's fun," JJ said. "A peek into what astronauts feel."

"That's what I'm afraid of."

"You're a dancer," Dyl pointed out. "Twirling should be a piece of cake."

"But I don't dance *blindfolded*, Junior. We have tricks to keep us from getting sick, but we have to be able to *see*." Song-Ye took a deep breath and nodded with obvious reluctance. "Okay. Whatever." She sat in the chair, put on the goggles and headphones, and let Zota twirl her. Growing pale, she clutched the arm of the chair with one hand, while pointing in the direction of spin with the other. Before the chair stopped, though, she yanked off the goggles and hunched forward, pulling in heavy breaths. "I'm going to be sick if this lasts any longer."

Zota's lips pressed together in a concerned frown. "Perhaps you should stay behind on the space-station mission, Cadet Park. The discomfort could be quite—"

"*Pfft*! I'll grit my teeth and get through it."

Tony looked surprised. "Boy, you guys sure like these Challenger Center simulations."

"Just wait," JJ told him.

Zota straightened and spoke with great intensity. "You are as prepared as you're going to be. Because you changed the future last time, you will be traveling to a time that's much like my own, but there will be differences… whether small changes or large ones, I cannot tell. This is unknown territory. Remember, the future is your choice. The decisions you make affect what is to come."

He led them out of the room toward the painted airlock door. He paused, looking at all of them with a concerned expression. "In my time, there were no survivors when Moonbase Magellan was destroyed. After the attack, the ISSC was Earth's watchtower, a place from which to monitor the Kylarn invasion—until the aliens took it over and used the space station against us. After that, we didn't have a chance."

Zota closed his eyes as if he didn't want to look at the cadets. "I did not know much about Earth's space program then. I watched the horrific battles and saw the violence the Kylarn unleashed, how many millions were killed…our cities, our monuments, our works of art, all destroyed. Fires raged for weeks and months across the continents. Refugees were everywhere." He opened his eyes, and he looked pale. "The Kylarn set up camps and began to perform experiments on prisoners."

"Maybe we've already changed that," King said. "We discovered the secret alien base much earlier, and we helped the Moonbase crew."

"We won't know what changed until we get there," JJ said. After hearing Zota's story, her heart was pounding, and she was even more determined than before. "Come on, I'm ready to go."

"Perhaps you can save more of the future," Zota said, "but remember, your primary mission is back *here*. None of those terrible events have happened yet, and if Earth can be prepared, then the aliens won't conquer us so easily."

Song-Ye said, "Maybe the Kylarn won't even try if we look like too much of a challenge."

Tony leaned toward JJ. "You never mentioned these simulations had such a *complicated* set-up! Good thing I've done enough live-action roleplaying that I catch on pretty fast. I just hope the high-tech stuff in the 'future' is believable."

"You won't be disappointed," JJ assured him. "Really. We're actually *going* to the future."

Overhearing, Dyl added, "This is our second time. For us, it's *back* to the future."

"Got it." A slow grin spread over Tony's face. "I'm glad I showed up today."

From a closet, the commander withdrew a set of blue jumpsuits similar to those worn by Challenger Center flight directors, but of a stretchier material. "Suit up so you're ready to join the space-station crew. He sized Tony up, then rummaged through the shelves for another jumpsuit. "This should fit you, Cadet Vasquez."

Zota stood in silence as JJ and the others pulled the flight suits on over their street clothes. JJ tugged on her sleeves and attached the Velcro fastenings. The jumpsuit had plenty of pockets and clips; she realized how useful that might be in zero-gravity while floating around inside a space station. She wouldn't want anything drifting loose and hitting her on the head, like the pubs bag had during her recent training flight.

Tony leaned over, shaking his head. He whispered, "You know how much I love role-playing games, but I can't believe this Zota guy is so into his own character!"

"It's all very real to him."

Zota opened the door of the Challenger Center's airlock chamber, where students participating in simulations were "transported" off to their assigned missions. In this case, JJ knew it would be the real thing.

The commander stood at the door, troubled. "One last thing—while I cannot personally return to the future because of the limitations of the Kylarn device, I was at least able to transmit a message on your previous mission. This time, however, we will be cut off from each other. Since the future is different now, I will have no way to communicate with you." His brows drew together in concern. "You're on your own until the mission has ended. Make this count."

"We won't let you down, sir," King said.

"Believe me, I'll do my best," Tony said.

JJ felt a new rush of anticipation, as she entered the airlock chamber.

After they were all inside, Commander Zota said, "Notice the handles." He indicated the walls of the chamber. "I suggest you hold on—the transition is likely to be even more disorienting than the Barany chair."

Song-Ye, Dyl, and King each grabbed a handle. JJ took the one closest to her and nudged Tony. "When Commander Zota says to hang on, you'd better hang on." He seemed amused and played along, resting a hand lightly on the grab bar. JJ saw that the rest of the Star Challengers were smiling.

Commander Zota closed and sealed the door.

FIVE

JJ's stomach gave a lurch, and it felt as if the floor fell out from under her, just as when the plane had dropped in the downdraft. She squealed with delight. "We're weightless!"

"Cool!" Dyl said. "*This* is not a problem!"

"Speak for yourself, Junior, I think I'm going to be sick," Song-Ye said.

The room was dimly lit, so JJ could barely see the faces of the others. Next to her, Tony gasped in surprise. "What is this, some kind of high-speed elevator? Or like NASA's vomit comet?" He chuckled. "Look at my legs floating! No wonder you guys were so excited about this simulator. It's pretty impressive!"

King started singing a song called "Free Falling."

JJ could barely feel the floor with her feet. She muttered, "Someone's got to try this out, and it might as well be me." She gave a slight push with her toes and sailed to the low ceiling, bumped it, and bounced off.

Tony was a split second behind her, ready to experiment. His arms windmilled, and he bicycled with his feet. "Whoa! I didn't expect *this*."

"Ouch!" Song-Ye yelled as Tony's foot connected with her stomach.

"Hey—knee in face," Dyl said. "This is a problem." Bright lights switched on, probably activated by a motion sensor.

"Everybody, take a minute to figure out where you are before we all get injured," King said. "Adjust to the new situation."

JJ looked around and suddenly discovered she didn't know which direction was up and which was down. This place no longer looked like the room they had started in. They were in a chamber about the size and shape of a hollowed-out school bus. Metal loops like drawer handles were distributed along every flat surface.

Tony tried to "swim" toward the wall, but made no headway.

King gave a low whistle.

"Not exactly what I expected a space station to look like, but this freefall thing is definitely cool," Dyl said.

"The best," JJ agreed. "Even better than being on the Moon."

Tony finally snagged one of the handholds and pulled himself closer to a wall—or was it the ceiling? "The Moon simulation, you mean?" He sounded completely confused. "This is so realistic. How long does it last?"

"As long as it needs to," JJ said.

"Yeah, wonderful, whatever." Song-Ye clutched a handhold, looking a little green. "Does anyone have some Dramamine? Because I'm definitely going to toss my cookies if this keeps up."

"Not a problem. We'll find you a space-barf bag." Dyl chuckled.

JJ's blond ponytail floated behind her head, as if she were a mermaid in water. Dyl's hair was fluffed out around his head, like a coppery lion's mane, and Song-

Ye's long black hair floated free in every direction, while King's close-cropped hair looked unchanged.

Tony ran a hand through his hair, which appeared puffier than normal. "How did they do this? It must be super expensive."

"Uh-huh," King said, "it's a space station."

"Yeah, yeah, I get it—it's supposed to feel like that. Just go with it."

JJ grinned over at him. "Told you it would be fun. Somebody's got to get this party started." She pushed off of the wall, giving herself enough momentum to float to the opposite side of the room. When she reached it, she rebounded and drifted past Tony in a slow-motion somersault.

"Let me try that." Tony, skilled in gymnastics and acrobatics, did a triple somersault, kicked off the wall, and spun his body in a tight circle, like an ice skater. "This is great!"

Song-Ye spoke in a shaky voice. "Glad you think so. Some of us are not having as much fun as the rest of you." The Korean girl tried "spotting" on a wall as she turned, a technique that ballet dancers used to keep from getting dizzy, but it didn't help settle her equilibrium. "I was disoriented enough in the Barany chair without any sight or hearing ... this isn't any better."

King got down to business. "Let's not forget why we're here. I'm guessing that must be an airlock." He pointed to a hatch at one end of the chamber, above them.

"Actually, there's an airlock on both ends of the module," Dyl said. "Piece of cake." He opened the nearest hatch and swung the thick metal door inward. "It's some kind of connector room." He shot inside. JJ was amazed at how well her brother moved, as smoothly as Tony doing acrobatics.

"Everybody in," King said, and they all crowded into the round chamber.

It was about the size of a normal elevator, and six hatches led from its walls, like some kind of game. "Pick a door, any door," JJ said.

Dyl closed and locked the first hatch behind them, while King peered through a viewport in the hatch closest to him. "This one just goes out into space."

Song-Ye checked another hatch. "This one, too."

"This one goes through to another module like the one we were just in, but it has a different setup," Tony said.

JJ said, "Since we can't step out into empty space, I vote for that one."

"Sure, why not?" Song-Ye still looked sick.

King started humming "Follow the Yellow-Brick Road" from *The Wizard of Oz*.

JJ and Tony opened the hatch, and they all floated through into a large, brightly lit module. This one was occupied.

A man and a woman in orange jumpsuits had been studying a videoscreen on the wall, and now they turned from it in surprise when they heard the hatch open. The woman pushed herself forward like a bullet, streaking past them to the hatch, which she slammed shut behind them. Her partner sailed into their path and anchored a foot to a metal bar on the floor. The man crossed his arms and studied them with suspicion.

JJ swallowed audibly. "So, I bet you wonder what we're doing here." She read the name patches on the workers' suits. The woman was named Napali, and the man was Kloor.

Kloor did not smile. "The thought crossed my mind."

From behind them, Napali said, "Boarding this space station without proper clearance is an indication of hostile intent."

Kloor gave a stern nod and spoke in a sour voice. "If it were up to me, you'd be out the airlock—but your arrival isn't entirely unexpected. The Stationmaster was actually hoping you would show up."

SIX

"What do you mean, hoping *we'd* get here?" JJ asked. "How would your Stationmaster know about us?"

Napali ignored the question. "I'm the security chief aboard this station, and I have my own questions. But that'll have to wait. The Stationmaster will want to see you immediately."

"Come with us," Kloor said

Following the crewman's lead, JJ pushed off the side of the module with her toes and used grab-handles to pull herself along. The feeling *was* like flying—it took almost no effort. She didn't think she'd ever get tired of this complete freedom of movement.

Dyl was enjoying himself almost as much as she was. He had a big goofy grin on his face as he moved along. He and King stayed close to Song-Ye, who looked ready to lose her breakfast. *That* was something JJ did not want to see in freefall! Tony, of course, still didn't understand what was really going on. He sent her astonished glances, trying to keep up. Even in the few short minutes they'd been here, their adventure had gone far beyond anything he could excuse as a simulation.

Napali herded them along from behind. "Why would anyone show up on a space station without clearing it through security? Official protocol requires me to 'disable' anyone who boards the ISSC without permission and treat them as a threat to Earth—especially in the current climate." She gave them a disapproving look.

"Believe me, we're not a threat," Tony said, not quite covering his grin. Lowering his voice, he asked JJ, "When does gravity kick in again? This is great!"

"Not for a long time, I think," JJ said honestly. "You'd better get used to it."

"But no simulation could last this *long*!" Tony argued. They passed through an airlock into a small chamber and exited through another airlock in a completely different direction.

"Here we are, the Central Command Module," Kloor said. "We just call it Central."

JJ pushed off and sailed through the doorway ahead of the others. She stared in delighted recognition at a woman who looked up from a console near the center of the module. Her eyes were golden brown, and her wavy chestnut hair was shorter than JJ remembered.

"Chief Ansari!" JJ tried to backpedal in the air, but momentum kept her moving forward.

As soon as Noor Ansari saw the Star Challengers enter the module, she released a strap that held her in place by the console and pushed herself over to greet them. She soared through the air like a circus acrobat, caught JJ, and steadied her. "Cadets, it's so good to see all of you." She nodded at Dyl, King, and Song-Ye, then hesitated a moment when she didn't recognize Tony, although she accepted his presence.

"Good to see you, too," Dyl said.

"You escaped from the moonbase then?" Song-Ye asked.

"What happened?" King asked.

Ansari responded with a puzzled look. Turning to Kloor, Napali, and two crewmembers who were watching curiously from their workstations, the stationmaster addressed them briskly. "Could I please have some time with the new arrivals? I need to debrief them."

Clearly mystified, the others retreated from the module with suspicious looks toward the newcomers. Security Chief Napali was reluctant to leave, but Ansari shooed her away. "Go—I'll provide information as soon as I have it."

When they were alone, Dyl swam through the air to give Ansari a hug. "Chief! It's such a relief to see you. We thought you were dead after the moonbase attack."

Ansari gave him a rueful look. "Not quite dead yet, though it was a close call on the Moon. And actually, it's *Stationmaster* Ansari now, not Chief."

King smiled. "Congrats on the promotion."

"It seems my experience on the Moon gave me unique qualifications to command the space station," Ansari said, studying their faces.

JJ cautiously said, "It's, uh, been awhile, hasn't it?"

"A whole year," Ansari said. "Yet you cadets don't look like you've aged a day. You *are* still cadets, are you not?"

Song-Ye spoke up. "That's what Commander Zota calls us. He has another name for our group too, but—" her voice drifted off, as she realized she might have said too much.

"Just call us cadets, that's easiest," JJ said, remembering Zota's admonition not to reveal too much. "We never heard what happened to you ... uh, after we got back to Earth."

"You mean your Commander Zota didn't know? The whole world was in an uproar to learn of the alien attack. Where have you been?"

Alarmed, JJ blurted, "That's ... classified. Unfortunately, when we're training, we don't get much news." It seemed a convenient excuse, because the real explanation would have sounded impossible.

Ansari nodded slowly, as if she had just realized something interesting. "We wondered if you had survived, as well. Our whole moonbase crew made it out using the emergency suits from the bunkers. There were a few injuries on the way back to the ISSC in the retrofitted supply ship, but we have you cadets to thank for the fact that we made it alive. The *Halley* won't be carrying passengers again, but it got us safely away from the Moon. Captain Bronsky and Dr. Romero will be happy to see you."

Song-Ye gasped. "They're here, too?"

Ansari smiled. "When I was appointed Stationmaster of the ISSC eight months ago, I asked them to join my crew." She rummaged through a wall cabinet and handed them each a pair of socks. "Put these on instead of your shoes. They're quite practical, and they are less likely to damage delicate instruments." While they changed into the socks, Ansari stowed their shoes in the cabinet.

Tony put a hand on JJ's arm to turn her toward him. "This is *real!*" he exclaimed in a loud whisper, as if he had just realized it. Unfortunately, he underestimated the amount of force it would take to turn her in zero-G, and JJ spun around and around, drifting toward a wall until she bumped it. JJ wasn't hurt, just a bit surprised by the unexpected twirling.

Ansari continued to fill them in on the situation. "In the year since the aliens attacked Moonbase Magellan, we haven't managed to get any new images of their base—it's all still a mystery. We've recently launched our first stealth probe, which will arrive there in two days, and we hope to get some valuable images. The whole world is scrambling to revive its space programs after leaving them to gather dust for so many years."

Just then a chirp sounded from a control panel, and a light flashed to indicate an incoming message. Ansari flashed Dyl a quick smile. "Cadet Wren, would you mind answering that for me? You were an excellent communications officer at the moonbase.

Dyl grinned. "Not a problem." He pushed a foot against one wall and sent himself sailing toward the console. He activated the comm. "We read you, CMC, over."

After a brief pause, a familiar voice with a British accent said, "This is Collaborative Mission Control to ISSC. Stationmaster, we've been trying to get some intel on that new cadet, but—hold on a moment—is that Cadet Wren? What the blazes are you doing there? Over!"

"Major Fox! You don't know how good it is to hear your voice," Dyl said. "Over."

A video screen flickered on above the communications station, showing Fox, resplendent in a charcoal military uniform. "Am I to understand that your sister and the rest of the cadets are on the space station now? I must admit, I was dubious, but Stationmaster Ansari thought you might arrive soon. Over."

"Yes, we're all here," Dyl answered. "Only there are five of us this time. Over."

On the screen, Fox nodded without surprise. "Ah, yes. The newcomer. Can you reveal anything about your mission this time? These are very serious matters. Over."

King glided over to hover next to Dyl. "I'm afraid we can't tell you much more than last time, sir, but we're willing to help in any way we can."

Fox's eyebrows lifted. "I see." He looked disappointed, but squared his jaw. "I have no idea whether to regard this development as encouraging or ominous. In light of your arrival, I have a bit more research to do. Please inform Stationmaster Ansari that I expect a preliminary report from her within four hours. Over and out."

Dyl's mouth hung open. "So, Fox is running Collaborative Mission Control? Well, I didn't see *that* one coming."

Ansari looked amused. "I wanted to see your reaction—and Fox's. That was the reason I asked you to answer the comm. After we escaped from the moonbase, no one could deny the destructive intentions of the aliens. Dozens of governments put together an international military force and space program. Because he was already in the military and worked with our civilian space agency, Major Fox was promoted to full-bird colonel and put in charge of the CMC."

King gave a low whistle. "So it's Colonel Fox now? Props to him."

"The military wanted someone in command who had direct experience with the aliens. Colonel Fox and I have a history of working well together—I can't think of anyone I'd rather have in charge down there, and even though I'm a civilian, he wouldn't want anyone else running Earth's only space station."

Song-Ye said, "At least *he'll* believe us when we tell him we're under attack by aliens." JJ remembered the skepticism from CMC administrators when they had initially reported the alien base on the far side of the Moon. "I mean, *if* we're under attack," she hastily amended.

Ansari nodded. "I'd better gather some information that I can report back to him in four hours." She propelled herself over to the main comm station beside Dyl and pressed a panel button. "This is Stationmaster Ansari calling an all-hands meeting. Everyone aboard the station, please report to the Mess Module in fifteen minutes. I repeat, this is an all-hands meeting. I expect everyone to attend."

A voice responded over the station-wide communication system. "Uh, Stationmaster? This is Kimbrell. The Sat Team's already here in the Mess. We were just starting a meal."

"Then you have just enough time to eat and freshen up before the meeting. Attendance is mandatory." She switched off and gave a sigh. "I hate to do this to them—that team has been working around the clock on the satellite we're about to launch." She shook her head as she saw their mystified expressions. "That's right, you've all got some catching up to do."

Tony ran a hand through his hair, looking completely at a loss. "Believe me, we know."

SEVEN

Stationmaster Ansari led them out of Central. "It may take you a while to learn your way around the space station and figure out how the modules are interconnected. Some people find it confusing, especially since there is no real sense of up or down." She pushed off with gentle ease and dove straight "up" through a hatch in what JJ thought of as the command module's ceiling. The modules didn't have—or need—any specifically defined floor.

JJ and her friends scrambled to follow, often overcompensating, bouncing off of walls and into one another, but generally moving in the right direction. JJ twirled around in the air, like a dolphin. "And I thought that spinning chair in the Challenger Center was disorienting."

She expected a quick response from Tony, but her friend was deep in thought about what he had learned so far.

Following Ansari's summons, the rest of the ISSC scientists, specialists, and military personnel would be gathering in the Mess Module for the all-hands meeting.

After leaving Central, the Stationmaster waited only a second in the node room—the elevator-sized chamber that connected modules together—before passing through a hatch on the right that led into another module. "Each node room has a diagram, so you can tell where you are."

"Or we could leave a trail of breadcrumbs floating behind us," Dyl quipped.

"Crumbs can be dangerous in microgravity," Ansari said, "especially if you inhale them. We have good filtration systems, but they can't handle everything that gets into the air."

The Star Challengers crowded after her into the node room and then passed through a long laboratory module that contained sealed glove-boxes, spherical experiment chambers, and numerous canisters and squeeze bottles of labeled chemicals, which were held in place behind webbing on shelves. Computer screens dotted the walls at several testing stations.

Ansari spoke like a hurried tour guide. "This is the Chemistry and Materials Science lab, or CMS, where our materials specialists grow crystals and microfibers." She cast a glance over her shoulder as they kept drifting along. "Originally, it was designed only for research and industrial applications, but now we're also trying to find innovative ways of defending ourselves against the alien threat. That's our highest priority—for the whole world."

"Anything good in the works?" JJ asked. "A prototype of some kind?"

Ansari reached the far side of the CMS module, grabbed the hatch frame that led into the next node room. "Our problem right now is that we have almost no information about the aliens. We don't know anything about their physiology, their biochemistry, what sort of air they breathe, what kind of planet they come from. More important for Earth's defense, we don't know their science, weapons, ships, basic technology—although we hope to gather some good intel on their base when the *Recon-1* probe gets there tomorrow. If only we had some hints … but for now we're still in the dark."

"They call themselves the Kylarn," King said, then responded to JJ's surprised look, "It can't hurt to give them some basic information."

"Where did you learn that?" Ansari asked.

"We … can't say," JJ answered.

Looking flustered, the Stationmaster passed through the connecting chamber and led them upward into another module, guiding them at a rapid clip. They went through a well-lit greenhouse and a moist-smelling Biosciences Module, then dropped down through another node room into Hab Module 2, where some of the station crew had their living quarters.

Song-Ye seemed queasy. "Now I know how Newton feels when he runs around in his hamster tunnels."

"The Mess Module's just up ahead."

"You have a whole module that's just a dining hall?" Tony asked.

"Not exactly. MESS is an acronym for Multiple Essential Station Services. The Mess Module is a combination of dining hall, recreation room, community area, and meeting room. We usually refer to it as the Mess. The members of the satellite team are eating there now. The Sat team has mostly finished prepping the Eye in the Sky satellite for launch." Ansari smiled as they floated into the Mess. "And *your* fellow team member is also there."

"Our team member?" JJ asked.

Before the Stationmaster could answer, JJ saw five crewmembers. Four had finished eating hot prepackaged meals and were placing the leftover components and scraps into recycler cabinets. Stationmaster Ansari greeted them. "This is our Sat team: civilians Lifchez and Kimbrell"—she pointed to two men in yellow jumpsuits—"and the military half of the team, Major Rodgers and Lieutenant Kontis." The man and woman in darker jumpsuits nodded hello.

As her friends floated in around her, JJ's attention was immediately drawn to the fifth person, a girl close to her own age, who looked out of place among the Sat team members. She had high cheekbones, hazel eyes with a fringe of long lashes, a light dusting of freckles across her fair skin, and pixie-cut auburn hair. She was dressed in blue like the Star Challengers.

The other girl's eyes locked on them like targeting lasers on a video game. "Stationmaster Ansari suggested we might be expecting visitors," the stranger said.

JJ was taken aback to see another teenager there on the station. Song-Ye and Dyl stared, while King said quietly, "Now this is interesting."

Tony had already experienced an avalanche of surprises. "Who's that?" He looked at JJ. "You didn't tell me there was anybody else."

Stationmaster Ansari turned to the Star Challengers. "Cadet Mira arrived two days ago and has been assisting us extensively ever since. She was quite surprised when I explained to her how four of you helped us at Moonbase Magellan. You're all part of the same team?"

"I assume so," the other girl answered quickly. "I was also unaware of other … team members."

"Are you a Star Challenger too?" Dyl blurted.

"Star Challengers? Is that what you call yourselves?" Mira raised her eyebrows and looked at Ansari. "As I told you, Stationmaster, our work is highly classified and compartmentalized. We must be from separate parts of our … project."

"Hmm, I assumed you had all met before," Ansari said.

"Maybe we need a few minutes to get to know each other," JJ said. "Is there someplace we could talk before the meeting starts?"

Stationmaster Ansari said, "Perhaps that would be best. I need to make some preliminary notes on my datapad, and the other crewmembers will take a while to get here. Hab 2 is adjacent to the Mess—Cadet Mira, would you please show our friends?"

Without commenting, the strange girl led the way.

EIGHT

The moment they were alone in the hab module, JJ turned to the other girl, asking excitedly, "Where are you from? How did you get here?"

The girl's hazel eyes darted from side to side, as if she were worried someone might be listening. Her voice held an edge of challenge as she dodged the question. "Where are *you* from?"

King spoke up. "I'd suggest that we all sit down and relax, but there's not much point in sitting when you're weightless." He pushed lightly against the nearest wall and glided toward Mira, holding out his hand. "So for now, I guess we should all just give each other some background."

Mira reached out dubiously and took his hand. King shook vigorously, which set them both moving, their whole bodies bobbing up and down like two people on an invisible seesaw. King released his grip, and the girl went one direction while he drifted in the other. "Sorry—I'm still not used to weightlessness!"

Everyone laughed, breaking the ice slightly. "The Stationmaster introduced you kind of fast," JJ said. "We didn't get your whole name."

The girl's eyes narrowed. "Mira—*just* Mira. That is already more than you need to know." She sounded wary. "You're aware of what's at stake."

JJ sighed. She couldn't tell if Mira was being difficult or merely cautious.

"How did you get here?" Song-Ye asked.

Mira ran her tongue along the inside of her lips to moisten them. "Most likely, just the same way you came."

Song-Ye said, "That's not an answer."

"The fact that you need to ask tells me that I shouldn't answer."

Tony spoke up. "Don't you think Mr. Zota would have told us if he'd sent somebody else here?"

"I don't know anyone named Zota," Mira said.

"Then I'm pretty sure you *didn't* get here the same way we did," JJ said pointedly. "We're asking who your commander is."

Mira's eyes did not meet hers. "No one commands me. I do have a guide, however: Mentor Toowun."

The Star Challengers exchanged curious glances. Dyl said, "So Commander Zota's not the only one?"

"But there *can't* be others like Commander Zota!" King whispered.

JJ thought the same thing, but if Zota had managed to escape into the past, why not others? Like Mentor Toowun. Zota's mission was to help the younger generation prepare for and prevent a terrible future. Did it make sense that the whole human race would need to trust its fate to just four or five Star Challengers, no matter how dedicated they were?

"Well, with such a big problem, shouldn't we be glad for all the help we can get?" Tony asked.

King nodded. "Saving the world's a big job."

"Where's your mentor from?" Dyl asked, "Or should I ask *when*?"

Mira's expression didn't change. "Those are both excellent questions."

"The plot thickens," Dyl murmured, looking intrigued by the girl.

"Which Challenger Center did you come through?" Song-Ye's voice held a hint of resentment.

Mira gave her a sharp look. "Again, your lack of knowledge indicates that I shouldn't answer. That information is on a need-to-know basis."

King gave a low whistle. "You're tough. Remind me to stay on your good side."

For an instant, JJ thought she saw Mira's lips curl upward ever so slightly, then the moment was gone. JJ had a million questions, but Zota had warned them not to reveal too much about themselves and their mission. Mira seemed to have similar instructions. The Star Challengers did not belong here in the future, and now was not the time to ask for too many details. Their questions had already told Mira quite a bit.

"But aren't we allies?" King went on. "Don't we have the same goal?"

Mira gazed around at them. "Is your purpose to change situations so that billions of humans won't need to die in the future?"

All of them nodded except Tony. "*Billions*? Isn't that a bit of an exaggeration?"

JJ winced. "I wish it were, but she's right. That's why we're here, too."

Mira focused on Tony. "How is it that your team knows this, but you don't?"

Tony ran a hand through his hair. "I'm new. I kind of joined this mission at the last minute."

The girl arched an eyebrow at him. "Last minute? Convenient."

"Not really. I'm still trying to figure out what's going on." Tony shook his head in disbelief. "What on Earth could kill billions of people?"

"Nothing on *Earth*," Mira said. "It was the Kylarn. I was not there when it happened, of course, but I know the stories. I've heard terrible descriptions that no one should have to hear, much less experience." Now her flat voice turned urgent. "Someone must have told you the stories—*that* part can't be a secret. It will happen not long from this time period.

"When the Kylarn come to take over Earth, humans will fight them with anger, frenzy, and fear—but not with intelligence. Millions and millions will be slaughtered by Kylarn laser shredders—like a mesh of hot wires that cut people to ribbons. Humans will try to retaliate, and the war will go on and on, while millions more die painful deaths—not just from the shredders, but from disease and starvation, until nearly two billion humans are dead." Mira's voice shook with emotion, and JJ thought she saw a shimmer of tears in the girl's eyes. For a second JJ wondered what would happen to tears in microgravity, then she pushed the thought from her head.

The other girl continued. "It's so stupid! They'll all die for nothing. They accomplish *nothing*!" She breathed deeply, calming herself. "But none of it has happened yet, so there's still a chance. I want to save as many of those lives as possible. I can't tell you much more than that."

"We're keeping things on the down-low, too," King said.

"But let's try to help each other out when we can, okay?" JJ said.

Mira agreed. Before they could discuss anything further, Stationmaster Ansari called for them. The all-hands meeting was about to start.

NINE

Crewmembers entered from four separate hatches in the module, pulling themselves hand-over-hand, bumping against the wall plates with their socks, moving as comfortably in the weightlessness as fish swimming about in a school.

When all of the ISSC crew was gathered in the Mess, Ansari made introductions. The Star Challengers had briefly met the Eye in the Sky satellite team, and now Ansari properly introduced the rest of the crew. "Dr. Harlan Kloor, our science officer, has earned more PhDs than any other person on Earth. He became so insufferable that there was no choice but to send him into orbit," she said with a rare teasing smile. "Actually, we're quite fortunate to have his expertise on board. And this is Security Chief Suri Napali."

"We've met," the woman acknowledged. "I am here to keep the station safe, but I doubt we'll see personal combat aboard."

Stationmaster Ansari continued around the circle. "Communications specialist Anton Pi and our astronomer Dr. Trina d'Almeida. The other two I believe you know?"

JJ and her friends were happy to see a familiar pair: Captain Bronsky, the Russian pilot who had flown the supply ship *Halley* to the moonbase during their previous adventure, and Dr. Cynthia Romero, the physician and biologist from Moonbase Magellan, who had worked closely with Song-Ye.

Most of the crew was baffled as to how five more teens had simply *arrived* at the International Space Station Complex without a ship. Mira looked pleased that her own presence no longer seemed as surprising.

JJ touched a fingertip to a bolted-down table to keep herself balanced and steady, since even small movements could send her drifting off in slow motion in uncontrollable directions. To her it seemed strange that the members of the ISSC crew were perfectly at ease sitting in all different orientations, some grasping handholds on the "ceiling" and facing downward, others on the "floor" looking up, still others facing inward from the walls. No matter which direction they faced, the center of the room was the focal point, where Ansari and the Star Challengers were.

Ansari called the meeting to order. "Obviously, we have plenty of questions, but let's keep discussion to a single track instead of ten."

"We all want to talk about the same thing, anyway," Bronsky said.

Dr. d'Almeida, the astronomer, shook her head. "It's simply not possible for six people to appear like rabbits out of a hat."

The science officer, Dr. Kloor, hung down from the top of the room. "It can't be *impossible*, since they're right in front of us. I'm eager to hear the explanation."

"If there was a shortcut to get up here to orbit, someone should have warned me," said Napali. "As Security Chief, I need to know if there's a back door I need to be guarding."

King sounded flustered. "I wish we had a scientific answer for you. But we're here—that's all we know."

"You really expect us to believe that you don't understand *how* you got to the ISSC?" said Lieutenant Kontis. She had generous lips, wide eyes, and glossy brown hair that she kept tightly secured in a regulation bun. Her question ended with an embarrassing burp, and she quickly covered her mouth.

"I can ride in a car without understanding how an internal combustion engine works," Dyl pointed out.

Kloor smirked. "*Internal combustion* engine? How quaint."

Ansari called for order again. "However they got here, these young people have joined us on the station, and I'm inclined to believe they can help us. They've proven themselves before."

"Excuse me, Stationmaster," said Pi, a muscular and cheery-looking man who reminded JJ of a young Jackie Chan. "I have practical concerns. We certainly have room on the station, and our solar-power arrays can provide enough power for additional crew, but our supplies will be strained by six extra people breathing the oxygen, drinking the water, and eating the food."

"I'll give up my rations if they taste anything like the meal we just ate." Major Rodgers, the Sat team payload specialist, wiped his mouth with an expression of distaste. "That was awful."

"We all seem to have lost our appetites," said Lifchez, a civilian scientist on the Sat team.

"That's why I couldn't eat," Mira said. "We're all tense, and we have important work to do. Suspicions and arguments only reduce the probability of success. We have to launch the Eye in the Sky satellite."

Dr. Romero added her support. "We just received a shipment of food supplies, so we'll do fine for now. Remember, I've seen first-hand what these young people can do. They'll earn their keep." She turned to look at Song-Ye, who had worked with her in the moonbase medical center. "How long will your group be here this time?"

The Korean girl shrugged with one shoulder. "Long enough to help."

Kimbrell, a civilian engineer who sat beside Lieutenant Kontis, muttered, "You kids don't know very much then, do you? Didn't you get a mission briefing?"

Stiff and formal, Mira crossed her arms over her chest. "I know you would all like to have explanations, but it's classified. We have our orders. This is a vital part of the mission, specifically relevant to Earth's response to the Kylarn. We are not authorized to say anything."

JJ didn't like the answer, but she was forced to agree. "Mira's right. We're not supposed to say much. It could"— she searched for the right words—"adversely impact the mission."

JJ was surprised when Major Rodgers nodded. "If we're not cleared for the information, then we don't have a need to know. That's for Earth scientists to decide."

"Besides, we all know who the real enemy is." Bronsky spoke up, defending the cadets. "It is as plain as the ears on your head. I was there when the aliens destroyed Moonbase Magellan—I barely survived myself. Stationmaster Ansari and Dr. Romero barely survived. These cadets were a great help. I say we must trust them."

"Colonel Fox down at CMC vouches for them as well," Ansari pointed out. "We're all here with a common goal: to find ways to protect humanity and defeat the aliens."

Dr. Kloor looked at the six young people who, scientifically speaking, should not have been there. "I've read the reports. We know the story of how these kids arrived at Moonbase Magellan just before it was destroyed." He pursed his lips. "Aren't we missing an obvious conclusion here? When these people show up, bad things happen. Trouble *follows* them. Since they're here on the space station, maybe it's just a matter of time before something goes wrong."

As if on cue, a piercing alarm shrieked from the station's intercom system.

TEN

Like birds startled from a roost, several crewmembers bolted from the Mess through the node room hatches, heading to their separate stations.

"Decompression alarm!" Ansari called.

The sound of the loud siren made Song-Ye's heart pound. Although queasy from being weightless aboard the space station, she was determined to fight and get over it. They had been here only an hour or so, and she hoped she would get used to it. Soon. With the emergency alarm going off, though, her gut clenched, and she had to breathe quickly through her nose to calm herself. "Is it a Kylarn attack?"

Pi reached a computer station in the Mess, scanned the screen. "There's been a breach in Hab 1—some sort of impact. Losing atmosphere at a rapid rate."

"Good thing everyone was here for the all-hands meeting," Napali said, "or there might have been crew sleeping in that Hab Module."

Ansari drew up beside Pi. "Has the hatch sealed?"

Pi nodded. "Automatically closed off at the node room, but we need to get the leak patched as soon as possible. Send the team out for an extravehicular activity."

"Looks like we'll have to suit up," said Lieutenant Kontis. "Time for the repair crew to do an EVA." She looked at her companions, Kimbrell and Lifchez. "A leak that bad should be readily apparent from outside. We'll see the air leaking. Which one of you wants to go with me?"

"We're all qualified, but ..." Lifchez drew a deep breath, and Song-Ye noticed beads of sweat on his forehead. "If it's all the same to you, Lieutenant, I'm not feeling too well. I might not be the best choice for a spacewalk."

Kimbrell also looked shaky and pale, but he said, "I don't feel so hot myself, but at least I feel better than *he* looks."

Lifchez groaned. Kimbrell and Major Rodgers simultaneously let out loud belches.

"None of you looks well," said Dr. Romero. "What are your symptoms? Maybe I'd better check—"

"No time for that, Doc!" Kimbrell said. "We've got an emergency here. Something's hit the station."

"I'm not at one-hundred percent either." Lieutenant Kontis took Kimbrell in tow. "So suck it up, and get moving. That leak isn't going to fix itself, and Hab 1 is losing air by the minute, so let's get to the Equipment Module and suit up."

"I feel fine," JJ volunteered. "We were all trained in spacesuits on the moonbase. Can we help?"

"An EVA spacesuit is different from a lunar suit," said Ansari. "We'll train you all—but not now."

Lieutenant Kontis ended the discussion. "We don't need the help—we'll do fine. This isn't a training mission."

Although she was willing to suit up and had definitely enjoyed going out on the lunar surface, Song-Ye was glad she would have more time to acclimate to the station. She thought of the meteor shower that had struck Moonbase Magellan and how they had been forced to duck underground into the shelters. "Was it a meteor strike?" she asked.

"Not likely," Ansari said as Pi continued to scan the screens. "Probably space junk."

"At least it's not an alien attack," said Lifchez, then he, too, let out a loud belch. "I don't suppose you have something to settle my stomach with you, Doc?"

"I do back in the Med Module," Romero said.

"What space junk?" JJ asked. "You mean we've just been bonked by … litter?"

"Over the years, the world's space programs left a great many discarded items scattered along the various orbits," said Ansari. "Spent fuel boosters, dead satellites, a lost tool or two, pieces of shrapnel—anything ranging from a couple of centimeters across to large items of equipment. Depending on their orbits, these chunks of space debris can collide with relative velocities of more than 50,000 kilometers per hour."

King whistled, and Dyl found the number impressive enough to jot it down on one of his notecards.

"According to estimates, more than half a million bits of space junk larger than ten centimeters in diameter are up here—with tens of millions of pieces smaller than that. It's one of our greatest risks."

During Ansari's explanation, Pi managed to mute the sirens, and Song-Ye let out a relieved sigh. The alarm lights continued to flash, though, so none of the crew could forget they were on an emergency footing.

The intercom crackled. "This is Lieutenant Kontis. We are in the Equipment Module, suiting up now. We expect to egress in fifteen minutes."

"Don't slack on safety, Lieutenant," Ansari said.

"Sounds like my Uncle Buzz," JJ murmured to Song-Ye. "Safety first."

"We're not taking any shortcuts, Stationmaster, but time is of the essence," Kontis replied. "However, Kimbrell and I are moving a bit slower than usual. That lunch isn't sitting well with either of us."

Dr. Romero was very concerned about the other two members of the satellite team. "Both of you look gray." She placed her palm against Major Rodgers's forehead, then pressed her fingers against the side of his neck. "You feel clammy, and your pulse is fast."

Rodgers waved her away with false cheer. "I can hold on until they seal off the breach. Plenty of time to give us all a once-over later." Romero mumbled something resigned about military officers needing to look tough.

Concerned but all business, Ansari suggested the crew return to Central in order to see and communicate with the outside team.

"I've got a full view from my observatory module," d'Almeida offered. "I can keep a lookout from there. Any of you are welcome to come along."

Major Rodgers decided to stay posted beside the controls for the ISSC's robotic arms that were mounted to the exterior of the station, in case the two space-walkers needed any assistance. As payload specialist for the satellite, Rodgers was the most proficient in using the complex remote-controlled robot arm.

Bronsky said, "I will also suit up if necessary. Aside from Lifchez, I'm the only EVA-trained backup."

Ansari led them through the maze of modules, through hatches and node rooms, bypassing Hab 1, which was sealed because of the leak. Song-Ye was glad to be moving again, because it distracted her from her unsettling space-sickness. She was pretty sure her own queasiness wasn't the same thing the five members of the satellite team were suffering. She was particularly worried to see the troubled look on Dr. Romero, who was normally very calm and cool.

Hovering beside her, Dyl reached out to poke Song-Ye gently on the arm, a teasing gesture that sent her floating toward the opposite wall. She pushed herself back in the right direction and made a face at him, but she could read his concern. "You all right?" he asked. "You look like you're about to take a final exam you haven't studied for."

"I'm fine, *Junior*." She realized she sounded testy, but she didn't mean it. "I never realized how much I appreciated gravity. This is like being seasick in three dimensions."

Pi arrived in Central first and clipped himself with a flexible strap to the communication station; he floated in midair, as comfortable as if he were sitting in a chair.

Over the intercom, Lieutenant Kontis reported, "Kimbrell and I have completed our suit-up procedures and are prepared to exit the hatch. Decompression complete in the chamber."

An external camera showed two bulky suited figures emerging from a large bay. JJ and Tony drifted over to one of the wide viewing windows in Central. "We can see them from here."

Dyl and King joined them. Song-Ye moved a bit closer, but felt unsettled by looking out into the starry blackness. The two figures outside moved forward, painstakingly making their way across the ISSC's hull. They pulled themselves along by handholds, tethered to the station like floating mountain climbers.

Tony's voice sparkled with excitement. "Don't you wish we could be out there?"

Song-Ye felt it best not to answer, but JJ sounded just as excited. "It could happen—just wait."

The two space-suited figures attached their tethers to another external hook, then moved forward again. "We see the leak now, Stationmaster—a tiny spray of atmosphere," Kontis said.

Her partner burped again, covered it with a cough, then said, "The impact point is no larger than a centimeter in diameter. We can patch it easily. What's the air pressure in Hab 1?"

Pi checked. "Seven point three pounds per square inch—we're down by about a third. We'd save a lot of air if you two could put that patch in place pronto."

"Going as fast as we can, Central," said Kontis, then took several audible gulps of air. "I'd like to get back inside as soon as possible. We're both encountering a bit of distress."

"What sort of distress?" Ansari asked. "We're checking your suit readings. All systems seem nominal."

"*Intestinal* distress. Remind me never to choose the mushroom curry lunch package again."

"I had the stroganoff, but I don't seem to be doing any better," Kimbrell added.

"Mine was just spaghetti and meatballs," Lifchez said, clutching his stomach as a cramp hit him. He drifted toward the control module wall, where he hung weakly onto a handle.

"This is a whole different level of emergency, Stationmaster," Dr. Romero said.

"Do you think it's food poisoning?" Song-Ye shuddered, remembering when she had endured a bout of Salmonella, the first and only time she'd ordered a buffalo burger medium-rare. It had tasted delicious, but within hours she suffered from cramps and then spent the next twelve hours in the bathroom with unending bouts of vomiting and diarrhea. Her mother had brought her some sport drinks to keep her electrolytes balanced. It had been one of the most miserable days of Song-Ye's life, and there was nothing for it but to stay hydrated and wait it out.

"No time to get sick until the job is finished," Kontis said. "Come on, Kimbrell, you know the drill."

The two figures moved painstakingly forward with their repair kit. They had several thick adhesive plates of various sizes. "A small one should do well enough here," Kontis said. "Four centimeters by four centimeters." Atmosphere continued to squirt out of the hole in silence, because space, like the Moon, had no atmosphere to carry sound.

The two astronauts' suit cameras showed the operations as the workers applied rapid-setting sealant from a tube, and pressed down hard on the metal patch to cover the small hole. "Seal is in place. That should stop the leak," Kontis reported.

Kimbrell added, "I'm applying a secondary layer of sealant around the edges. It'll be good as new. We can start testing the integrity and pump atmosphere back into Hab 1, then add a reinforcement patch on the interior wall."

"That part's not our job. We're finished out here," Kontis radioed back. Her voice sounded breathless and weak. "We need to end this EVA as quickly as we can."

"Return to the Equipment Module, both of you," Ansari said. "That's an order. Dr. Romero will see you as soon as you're back in."

"Vomiting in zero-gravity could make quite a mess," King pointed out.

Tony grimaced. "I did not need that mental picture."

"Gross. Let's hope we don't have to verify King's theory from experience," Dyl said.

"Ick!" JJ said. "I mean that as an acronym."

"Insanely cruel knowledge," Song-Ye said.

On the intercom, the two astronauts fell ominously silent as they concentrated on pulling their way along the tethers back to the airlock hatch. "Entering the bay now," Kontis finally said. "Seal the hatch behind us! Pressurize."

"Vomiting in a spacesuit can actually be quite dangerous," Ansari explained to the teens.

In the Equipment Module, the astronauts seemed to be scrambling, shouting to each other, breathing hard. "Get the helmet off, quick!"

Song-Ye looked with alarm at the nearest intercom speaker as they heard loud retching sounds.

Ansari barked, "Lieutenant Kontis, Kimbrell, report. What is your status?"

Kontis finally reported, sounding weak, her voice rough. "We got the helmets off just in time, Stationmaster, but I can now report that microgravity barfing is not pretty. I can also verify that Kimbrell did indeed have the beef stroganoff, while I had the mushroom curry. Right now, though it's a bit hard to separate them."

"Ick!" Dyl said. Song-Ye felt her stomach twitch with sympathetic nausea.

Major Rodgers and Lifchez let out moans of distress as they hunched together, drifting near a wall of the control module. Rodgers said in a wobbly voice, "Sorry to interrupt the festivities, my friends, but I'm about to be ill. Doc, I'll take you up on your offer to go to Med." Lifchez moaned his agreement.

"That does it." The doctor's stern voice allowed no room for argument. "I'm taking the whole Sat team to Medical, Stationmaster. Something's not right here."

"Better ... hurry." Lifchez covered his mouth, looking green behind the gills. Dr. Romero and her queasy patients scooted through the hatch heading toward the medical module.

Pi looked concerned. "That's all four members of the satellite crew, Stationmaster. We're supposed to launch the Eye in the Sky tomorrow—it's vital."

"It definitely sounds like food poisoning," Ansari said. She turned toward Mira. "You ate with them, Cadet. Do you feel any ill effects?"

"I ate very little," she said. "I didn't have much of an appetite."

"Kimbrell and Kontis, as soon as you're out of your suits, get to Medical."

"Aye, Stationmaster," the lieutenant said with a quiet groan.

"It sounds like Dr. Romero will have her hands full. I'd like to help her, if you don't mind," Song-Ye said. Ansari gave her an approving nod.

"Uh, one more thing?" Lieutenant Kontis said over the intercom. "Somebody better bring handheld vacuums to the Equipment Module to take care of the, um, mess in the air."

"Volunteers?" Ansari turned and looked directly at Dylan and King.

JJ elbowed her brother, who drifted sideways while she floated in the opposite direction.

"Uh, okay, we ... volunteer?" Dylan said unconvincingly. "No problem."

"Uh-huh. We'll get that cleaned up for you, ma'am." King seemed amused by Dyl's discomfort. He started singing a song about a carwash under his breath.

ELEVEN

After he and King finished cleaning up the Equipment Module, Dyl joined Song-Ye in helping Dr. Romero with the queasy crewmembers in Medical, which had rarely seen more than two patients at a time in the history of the International Space Station Complex.

The Medical module looked clean and spare, exactly as Dyl had always imagined a futuristic space station would look. The white walls looked like ceramic, although the panels felt warm to his touch. Storage cabinets, instruments, and readouts were built into the smooth material. The place reminded Dyl of sickbays in the science fiction shows he loved most.

Simple examination tables were firmly attached to the module walls. "Why do you need beds?" Dyl asked. "Wouldn't your patients be more comfortable if they just floated around?"

Dr. Romero had guided a groaning Kimbrell to one of the beds and strapped him in place with crash webbing. "It's hard to treat patients who float around at the slightest touch."

"I can see how that would be a problem."

Song-Ye helped Lieutenant Kontis onto an examination pallet and strapped her to it. Though the Korean girl still looked a bit spacesick, it was nothing compared to what the ill crewmembers were feeling.

Lights blinked on video screens above each patient. Doctor Romero pointed to the status. "Each medbed measures the patient's vital signs—blood pressure, temperature, pulse rate, levels of blood gasses, and so on."

Lifchez started to make retching noises on his medbed. Dyl grabbed a vacuum nozzle and moved away from the side of the module to help the man, who looked like he was about to throw up again. He arrived with the apparatus just in time to vacuum the barf out of the air by Lifchez's head before it could float around and make more of a mess.

Lifchez mumbled. "Sorry, but ... that's not the end I'd be most worried about, if I were you."

"Oh," Dyl said, as the meaning sank in. "I—uh, *this* is a problem."

"You'll have to get him to the toilet," Dr. Romero said, as Kimbrell started to retch again. "As you can see, I've got my hands full here. Fortunately, one of the station's six toilets is right here in Medical." She pointed to a small cubicle built into the wall.

Lifchez's forehead broke into a cold sweat as Dyl guided him toward the cubicle. Dyl had been on the station for less than two hours and didn't even know how to use a bathroom in zero-G. The military man grabbed a handle beside the toilet seat and turned. "Thanks. I can take it from here," he said in a shaky voice and pulled the privacy shield closed.

Dyl breathed a sigh of relief, since he would have had no idea how to help. "How exactly does that thing work, anyway?" He floated back over to where Song-Ye and Dr. Romero tended the rest of the Sat team.

Dr. Romero said, "It takes some getting used to. There's no gravity up here to help with the, um, *flow* of everything, so we can't use water in the toilets. The system is based on air flow."

"As in, a vacuum cleaner?" Song-Ye asked.

"Pretty much," Dr. Romero said. "You also have to use foot loops, handles, and straps to keep yourself in place or you might drift in unwanted directions. When you're in position, you activate the air suction to carry away waste. At the front of the toilet there's a suction hose for liquids. And there are specialized adapter funnels—one for women and one for men."

"Right now, uh, I think I can hold it a while longer," Dyl said.

Romero finished analyzing the patients' blood work and shook her head in surprise to discover that each of the four sick members of the satellite team had fallen ill with the food poisoning known as Salmonella.

Once Dr. Romero discovered what had caused the illness, she could better treat the Sat team members. "In the body, the Salmonella bacteria produces a poisonous byproduct, a toxin, that makes patients extremely sick. They'll recover just fine," she said, to everyone's relief. "But they'll need a few days of rest before they're back to full health. What I don't understand is how it could have gotten into four separate food packs like that ... unless there's something wrong with our preservation systems, but that doesn't seem possible."

More importantly, she was worried about a continuing outbreak. "Before we eat again, we'll have to test each of the packages to make sure the rest of our food supply is safe."

"Is that something we can help with?" Song-Ye asked.

Romero looked at her patients and let out a sigh. "Absolutely. If any other parts of our food supply are contaminated, it would be a complete disaster for the ISSC. We're already at a minimal active crew complement—in fact, if we didn't have you cadets to help, I don't know how we'd finish even our basic work."

Dyl and Song-Ye spent hours testing small samples from the food packets in the Mess module. After careful analysis, they found two more contaminated with Salmonella. Dr. Romero quickly sealed away those packets so no one else would get sick.

The patients looked at the packages with accusing glares. Lifchez groaned and didn't even want to read the labels.

"At least we've verified the safety of the other meals. We can have lunch now," Dyl said.

Song-Ye remained concerned. "That doesn't explain how they got contaminated in the first place, though."

After an exhausting day, the Star Challengers were assigned a sleep shift. Ansari showed them to an empty set of compartments in the repressurized Hab 1. "This will be your home sweet home, for as long as you stay here." She let them each choose their own private area.

"Everyone has a personal sleep station, a small compartment where you can get some privacy. Sleep stations are rather compact, but each one has a desk and lamp, nets to stow your clothes in, and a sleeping bag."

"So we get to go camping in space?" King said. He was an Eagle Scout, after all.

"I'll make s'mores," Dyl offered.

"The bags are sleep *restraints* more than anything else," Ansari said. "Just cloth with a stiff pad on the back. They keep you from floating around and hitting the walls while you sleep. When it's time for bed, you just shut your door and zip yourselves in for a good night's rest. Actually, it's not as easy to get used to sleeping in microgravity as you might think. We supply eye masks and earplugs, but it's still a strange sensation."

"As long as no one tries to spin me around in a chair, I'll deal with it," Song-Ye muttered.

"Living in space doesn't take much physical effort," Dr. Romero said the following day. "So we have to exercise to stay healthy. It's my job to keep track of the mass, bone density, and muscle tone of everyone on this space station. I require every member of the crew to put in at least two hours a day in the fitness module while they're stationed here in orbit. Otherwise their muscles and bones would deteriorate in microgravity."

Dyl wiggled his legs, enjoying the freedom of movement. "How hard can it be to run or ride a bike up here?"

She pointed out a magnetic treadmill. "That's called a 'colbert,' after the one on the original International Space Station. You wear straps and restraints to keep yourself secure against the equipment while you exercise. Between resistance exercises, the colbert, and the stationary bicycle, the crew stays pretty fit." She looked at the two of them. "Have you noticed any physiological differences in yourselves since you arrived?"

"My head feels all stuffed up," Dyl said. "And I have a runny nose." He had also noticed within the first few hours of their being aboard the ISSC that all of his friends' eyes looked swollen, their faces rounder. "Song-Ye is looking pretty plump in the face. Maybe she ate too much yesterday," he teased.

She shot back, "Listen to Mr. Puffy Cheeks, *pfft*!"

Romero nodded. "Perfectly normal. Gravity isn't keeping your body's fluids where they would normally be. In microgravity, your heart doesn't have to work as hard to circulate blood, so your body doesn't need as much fluid. In the next few days, you'll pee away what you don't need, and then you'll feel normal."

After Dr. Romero had adjusted the colbert, Song-Ye tried out the treadmill.

"Being in space for a long time can cause physiological problems for humans," Dr. Romero continued. "Space programs have been studying the effects since the first orbital flights, and then extended stays aboard the Soviet Mir space station, SkyLab, and the original International Space Station. One of the ISSC's most important areas of research is to learn how humans can live for long periods of time in space."

Dyl shook his head. "I have a feeling the Kylarn don't want us to feel welcome out here for an extended stay."

TWELVE

"Well, I know why *I* volunteered for this task," King said, raising an eyebrow at Mira before staring down at the electronic star charts. They were working together in the observatory module. "I'm an amateur astronomer, and I worked with Dr. Wu before on his charts. It's already interesting to me. The question is: What are you doing here?" It was a friendly query, not a challenge.

Mira moistened her lips and thought for a moment. King was sure the girl would give him the brush-off, but she surprised him. "I could claim that I like astronomy too, but you'd see through that right away, so there's no point. For now, let's just say I have an interest in … heavenly bodies." Her lips curled into a teasing smile, and her eyes locked with his.

King took a quick breath of surprise. Was she *flirting* with him? The tune of an old song, "Can't Take My Eyes off of You" flashed through his mind, and he quickly decided against humming it. "So, we have that in common, then," he teased her back.

Just then, Dr. d'Almeida glided in. "Dr. Wu's message this morning requested that you go over the images that he sent, Cadet King. Did you find the charts?"

"Yes, Ma'am, I believe we have them all," King said, pointing down at the screen. "It's hard to believe that it takes days or weeks to make each of these sky survey pictures. When I worked with Dr. Wu on the Moon, we used video images, but we used printed ones, too, for the blink test."

Dr. d'Almeida chuckled. "Dr. Wu is a brilliant astronomer, and he has some eccentricities. One of them is that he enjoys the feel of *real paper* in his hands. But as you can probably guess, dealing with hardcopy is impractical on the space station."

"Clearly," Mira said. "You can't even use paperweights to keep things in place."

"There are other ways, of course," d'Almeida said. "We have vacuum display boards, with tiny pinholes that draw in small amounts of air to keep lightweight objects in place."

"Huh," King mused, "like a reverse air-hockey table."

D'Almeida didn't seem to hear him. She continued. "Or magnetized sheets, or a tacky backing."

"Like sticky notes," Mira observed.

"But using the display screen is by far the simplest method. You can still do the blink test on screen, of course." D'Almeida touched the display table and flicked a finger back and forth. The projected deep-sky image changed from one starfield to another and back again. "But if you two have this in hand, I can get back to my other work in the observatory dome. Sometimes a real astronomer needs to look at the stars with her own eyes." With that, Dr. d'Almeida pushed off and zoomed to the far end of the module and the telescope enclosure, all the while singing softly in a foreign language. Apparently, she wasn't used to having other people in the module with her.

"Portuguese folk song," Mira pointed out. She lowered her voice to a conspiratorial whisper. "Maybe Wu isn't the only eccentric astronomer."

"Huh," King said with a smile. "Well, we all have a few things that make us different. Besides, some of us happen to think that a little bit of music makes the day go better." He started humming "Whistle While You Work" and flicked a finger on the display screen to switch back and forth between two images. He saw no important changes and switched to another pair of images, then another, then another. He settled into a rhythm, and after a few minutes Mira took over, switching from image to image.

"It seems like a pointless exercise, doesn't it?" she said. "They all look pretty much the same—a bunch of light dots on black."

King kept his eyes glued to the screen, alert for any differences. If one tiny star moved while the rest of the points remained the same, it would pop out like a jumping flea. "I can understand why Wu thinks it's important, but with the Kylarn threat, I guess looking for asteroids and comets has been put on the back burner."

At the moment, the station's crew, as well as most people on Earth, were particularly anxious to see the upcoming results of the surveillance probe, *Recon-1*, which had been launched before the Star Challengers arrived at the ISSC. The spy probe would capture images of the alien base on the far side of the Moon; it was due to arrive and send back its first pictures later that day. King wasn't surprised that tedious asteroid searches received little fanfare.... On the other hand, they all had to wait a few hours until *Recon-1* arrived at its destination. He wanted to do this for Dr. Wu in the meantime.

Bending over the screens, he spotted a flicker of change between one image and another. "There! Like that."

"I didn't see anything," Mira said. He wasn't sure she had even looked.

He flicked the image back, pointed to a spot, then switched to the original starfield again, pointing to another place. "See that? The dot moved."

"If you say so." Her voice sounded cool and distant.

"Take my word for it, we're making progress."

THIRTEEN

No one had gotten a glimpse of the Kylarn outpost on the far side of the Moon since JJ's previous mission to the future, when King, Major Fox, and she had discovered the bizarre alien military base being built in secret. After the destruction of Moonbase Magellan, Earth's space programs—now with the support of countless governments—had scrambled to put together a probe in order to get a snapshot of what the Kylarn were doing over there.

The private International Collaborative Space Agency, or ICSA, had relied on old technology in its space programs for years, and they simply had nothing ready that could serve as a spy probe to the Moon. It had taken most of a year, but finally the pieces were coming together.

"We know the Kylarn have been watching us, but until today we had no way to watch them back," Stationmaster Ansari said. "Now we have our own probe."

Inside Central, JJ waited with King, Tony, and the mysterious Mira. Dyl and Song-Ye were still helping Dr. Romero take care of the sick crewmembers in Medical.

"Even with the whole Sat team laid up with Salmonella, we need to find some way to launch the Eye in the Sky monitoring satellite—and soon," Mira pointed out. "I've trained with the team, so I can help."

Ansari considered. "That's possible, Cadet. But for today, let's see what *Recon-1* can show us."

The Russian pilot gave a gruff snort. "Eye in the Sky will keep watch from a safe distance, but my probe will go right to the alien base! We'll see how their secret outpost has changed over the past year." Bronsky had an almost fatherly attitude toward *Recon-1*, since he had built it himself, converting the battered old *Halley* for one last mission.

Bronsky had been the pilot of the supply ship that traveled from the ISSC to the Moon and back, delivering food and equipment, exchanging personnel. On its previous routine flight, the ship had passed over the far side of the Moon, where the Russian pilot was the first to spot the alien complex. When the *Halley* tried to make contact, the Kylarn had opened fire, forcing a crash landing from which Bronsky and his copilot had narrowly escaped with their lives. The discovery of the outpost stirred up the aliens, though, and they had destroyed Moonbase Magellan. The crewmembers barely made it back home in the repaired supply ship.

Afterward, the *Halley* had been decommissioned, too damaged to haul passengers again. It was Bronsky himself, working with satellite team members Lifchez and Major Rodgers, who had refitted the old spacecraft and turned it into an automated ship packed with observation devices: *Recon-1*. Today, the probe would reach its destination after a slow, stealthy journey.

"What's the difference between the probe and the Eye in the Sky satellite?" Tony asked.

"What's the difference?" Bronsky said, sounding offended. "*What is the difference?*" He shook his head.

"Eye in the Sky will be launched to an orbital stable point between Earth and Moon. It will keep watch from afar, but my *Recon-1* is a real spy! It sneaks right up to the alien base and shows us what they are really doing!"

"Unless the Kylarn see it first," JJ said. "Won't they just shoot it down? They've already proved they don't like to be spied on."

The Russian frowned. "That is a possibility, but we have taken precautions. My probe was launched from this station and drifted on course to the Moon, completely silent. Maybe the aliens will not notice."

Stationmaster Ansari said, "Both the *Recon-1* probe and the monitoring satellite are vital for collecting information. The more data we have, the better our chances against the aliens."

"*Recon-1* has entered lunar orbit," Pi reported from his station. "Radio silence will last close to an hour." JJ knew that while *Recon-1* orbited above the location of the Kylarn base on the lunar far side, the Moon itself would block all signals. But all the while, the probe would silently take images of what it saw.

Watching Pi at his station, she wondered if Dyl would ever get to take a turn as the Communications Officer for the ISSC, as he had at the lunar base. For now, her brother seemed content to help Song-Ye and Dr. Romero.

The Russian captain clapped his big hands together. "Soon enough we will learn what our alien friends have been up to."

"If they were our friends, we wouldn't have to be so worried about them," King remarked.

Ansari floated near the control screens, her dark eyebrows drawn together. "*Recon-1* will approach in low-power mode, no transmissions. Passive recording only while it's in radio silence, but once it comes back into range after going around the Moon, the probe will transmit its data in a burst."

Colonel Fox had sent an all-systems-go approval from CMC, and everyone on the space station and on the ground waited eagerly for the first images. JJ and Tony crowded together near one of the screens, while King and Mira floated in front of another screen. JJ found that she was holding her breath and let out a long exhale.

It was a very long hour.

Mira continued to watch intently. "The Kylarn won't simply be biding their time and waiting for us. We should see significant changes from the old images."

"Or maybe they just packed up and went home," Tony said.

"Not much chance of that," JJ muttered. She thought for the thousandth time, *If only Earth had spent more time looking outward at the space neighborhood, the Kylarn would never have caught us by surprise.... We would have been ready!*

"The probe is due to exit from the Moon's radio shadow soon," Pi said. "We'll receive the first images in a few minutes."

Bronsky waved a triumphant arm so hard that he lost his hold on the wall and drifted about until he bumped into something that he could use to nudge himself back to a handhold. "And they said *Halley* would never fly again after we returned!" He let out a snort of indignation.

A tense hush filled Central. JJ wondered if they would ever see the probe again, or if the aliens had destroyed *Recon-1* as soon as it tried to take secret surveillance images. They would find out in a few seconds. The chronometer ticked down.

"There it is!" JJ was the first to shout as she watched the monitor. A blip appeared at the edge of the Moon, orbiting around from the far side. "The Kylarn didn't destroy it!"

"*Recon-1* is now in contact, activating its broad-bandwidth burst transmission," Pi reported, his voice raised with excitement. "First signals coming in."

JJ knew that the probe had recorded a wealth of images and then raced away from the alien base. Now that *Recon-1* had emerged from radio silence and reestablished contact, the computers onboard were sending a fast transmission, like a quarterback throwing a football.

"Receiving infrared images …" Pi said, grinning. "Radar images … ultraviolet."

The visual data flowing across the screens painted a remarkable picture—the view that *Recon-1* had recorded half an hour ago as it tiptoed over the alien outpost. Every second, each image, gave them more information that could be used to fight the invaders.

As the screen resolved itself in the wide-angle camera shots, JJ gasped. Previously, the size of the alien outpost had been awesome—now it was three times as large! The Kylarn base had grown into a nightmarish amusement park of domes and tubes, mine shafts, alien rail cars, and robotic walkers that scurried about like metallic termites. She could see factories and glowing lights, strange geometric towers that climbed higher than the crater walls and connected to one another with wires and conduits.

And *ships*—dozens and dozens of alien craft on launch pads. JJ recognized spacecraft like the ones that had bombarded Moonbase Magellan … and other small vessels that looked like polished metal starfish.

"*Recon-1* was taking images on the fly, but there seems to be no response so far." Bronsky sounded immensely pleased. "Maybe the aliens did not notice our ship."

"Maybe the aliens aren't worried about us," Ansari said in a disheartened voice. "After all, we couldn't defend the moonbase when they attacked, and we haven't gone back there in a year. Maybe the aliens don't think we're capable of mounting any response."

"Realistically, what response can Earth make?" Mira asked in an edgy tone. "They're ten times more advanced than humans are."

Three of the ominous starfish ships rose up from the launchpads and began to spin like ninja throwing stars. Like predators on the hunt, the alien craft streaked off after *Recon-1*, twirling all the while.

"Uh-oh, they spotted the probe after all," JJ said. "These pictures were a few minutes old."

"But the probe survived and made it around the Moon," King said.

"Until now, at least." JJ looked at the tactical trace on another screen, which showed the orbital path of the probe. On the recorded images, *Recon-1* raced away from the alien base, heading toward the lunar horizon where it could send its desperate transmission, but the starfish-vessels closed on it.

"I think they mean business," Tony said.

"They must be on their way right now," Bronsky said with a sinking feeling. "It is over, I'm afraid."

The last images they all saw were the whirligig alien craft closing in. JJ knew the clunky, patchwork probe could not possibly outrun them. Bright white energy blasts sparked from the tips of the metal starfish arms … and then, in a burst of static, the screen went blank. JJ winced.

Dr. d'Almeida had directed her telescopes toward the Moon, and now she recorded images of the alien star-fish ships leaving the wreckage of the probe, turning, and racing back to the far side of the Moon, where they disappeared from view again.

Stationmaster Ansari let out an angry sigh. Bronsky's eyes filled with tears, which broke free when he blinked and drifted around Central like tiny transparent pearls in the weightlessness. "She was a good ship, and she served us to the last."

Ansari tried her best to sound reassuring. "The mission was a success. Those images will be vital for our planning."

"Planning for what?" Tony asked. "Anybody got a brilliant idea?"

"Across the whole human race, someone *must* have a brilliant idea," JJ said, and she meant it.

A transmission came in from CMC. On the screen, Colonel Fox said, "We received the initial recon information we had hoped for, and our experts will begin studying the data immediately." He cleared his throat, sounding all-business. "Stationmaster Ansari, now it's even more imperative that the Eye in the Sky is launched on schedule. It will provide a vital early warning of Kylarn activity on the Moon. We've got to get the satellite up to the Lagrange stable point. Will it be launched on schedule?"

Ansari looked uncomfortable. "The entire Sat team is still suffering from food poisoning, Colonel. They are in no condition to go back to work."

"All four of them?" said Fox. "Are you sure no one else is qualified to do the final pre-launch check?"

"I'm qualified," Mira said. "I worked with the team for two days to set up the system. There's a datapad checklist. I am confident I could get the Eye in the Sky ready for launch. Let me handle it."

"We'll volunteer, too," JJ said. She and her class had done a similar task during their Challenger Center mission. While this was a far more complex situation, she knew that Commander Zota would want them to try.

"Yes, we'll help." King nodded. "The mission is the most important thing."

Mira seemed uncomfortable. "That's … not necessary."

"I know a bit about electronics, and it's always useful to have a backup," King insisted. Though the other girl frowned, she did not press her argument.

JJ leaned closer to the communication screen. "We'll get the Eye in the Sky launched on time, Colonel Fox—you can count on us."

The British officer lifted his chin. "I'm inclined to let them try it, Stationmaster Ansari. We know the capabilities of those young people."

"I concur," said Ansari. "Cadets, the satellite mission is yours."

FOURTEEN

The mood aboard the ISSC was glum after the Kylarn destroyed the *Recon-1* probe. Now, JJ was sure that the aliens would be alert to stop any further observation probes sent directly to the Moon.

The Eye in the Sky satellite, on the other hand, would be in a position from which its high-resolution telescope could watch for any sign of aliens heading toward Earth—and keep a distant eye on the base. The satellite would be launched to a gravitationally stable point along the path on which the Moon orbited the Earth.

Dr. d'Almeida showed JJ, King, and Tony a diagram of the Earth-Moon system. "They're called Lagrangian Points," she said, "specific places in the Moon's orbit where the gravity of the Earth and Moon effectively cancel each other, so a satellite can sit there, completely stationary. We're most interested in the point named L-4, a spot that is sixty degrees ahead of the Moon as it orbits the Earth. If we can place the Eye in the Sky satellite there, it will be safely far away from the alien base, but we can still keep an eye on the lunar farside. We'll be able to get a warning as soon as the Kylarn decide to move."

"Like a lookout tower," JJ said.

The astronomer nodded. "A good analogy. But the satellite will be very far away from any human intervention. We have to make certain it functions properly."

"That's our job," King said.

When Lifchez heard that JJ, King, and Mira had been assigned to complete the final preparation checklist for launching the Eye in the Sky satellite, the Sat team leader tried to crawl out of bed in Medical, though he was still deathly ill. In the microgravity, this amounted to the patient unstrapping himself from the medbed and squirming out into the middle of the room, where he was unable to stop himself from spinning—which only made him feel more nauseated.

Fortunately, Song-Ye came in and found Lifchez, grabbed his arm and guided him back to his bed, where she strapped him down, ignoring his weak struggles. "I need to be there for the satellite launch!" he protested. "I've got to check all the systems."

Dr. Romero pulled herself into the Med module and hurried to the bed. She gave him a scolding cluck. "In your condition, you probably couldn't see the result numbers straight anyway."

"Don't worry, JJ and King will figure it out," Song-Ye said. "You can trust them."

Lifchez's further arguments came out as little more than moans.

On the other side of the Medical, Major Rodgers also struggled on his bed. "Checking the satellite isn't good enough. We need the robotic arm to launch it—it's a very complicated operation, and I'm the only one qualified." The payload specialist held out his hand, palm flat and fingers outstretched; his whole arm was shaking.

"Needs a steady touch, and that certainly isn't me." He let out a long sigh.

"Then someone else will have to do it," Dr. Romero said. "You're in no condition."

"Who else?" Rodgers said. "It takes quick reactions, familiarity with automated controls for waldo arms, and steady guidance. No one else has time to learn it, especially now that the whole Sat crew is down." He winced and pressed a hand against his stomach.

"I bet Tony can," Dyl said. "He's a whiz at video games, can operate all kinds of complicated joysticks and hand controls—and he even studies robotics. He won a science fair project by building and controlling his own robot."

Rodgers did not look convinced, but stared again at his shaking hands. "I can train him from here, if Dr. Romero lets me use one of the screens. We may as well give Cadet Vasquez a shot. Let's see what he can do."

When JJ and King pulled their way into the equipment module to go over the satellite checklist, Mira had already started without them. "I was wondering when you would get here." The other girl sounded impatient. "Stationmaster Ansari gave me clearance to begin the prep."

"We're due to launch in two hours," King said. "That should be plenty of time to check and double-check all systems. No mistakes this time."

"No, no mistakes." Mira looked as if she wanted to say more, but kept her words to herself. "I've already inspected the propulsion systems and attitude-adjustment thrusters, and I was about to verify the optics." She made it sound like she didn't need the other two at all.

JJ pulled out a datapad that held the checklist. "We should all three go through every one of the systems as a triple-check."

"Works for me," King said.

The refrigerator-sized satellite hung in the middle of the equipment module, tethered in place. The three floated around it on all sides, moving from top to bottom, and all the way around its diameter. King opened the metal covering of an electronics panel and tested the circuits one by one to make sure all were connected properly and functional.

JJ ran a self-test on the logic boards and checked the power systems. While she and King occupied themselves with small talk, Mira remained intent on the optical-imaging systems, telescopes, and sensors. She certainly wasn't overly friendly.

"We did a mission just like this in the Challenger Center," King said. "I had to hook up and test the circuits. It's the same sort of procedure—and I understand it a lot better now that I took that Intro to Electronics class online."

"I never thought I'd get my hands on an actual satellite," JJ said, moving to the next panel. "This is a lot bigger than Sputnik, the first satellite ever launched. That was only about the size of a beach ball." The Soviet launch of Sputnik in 1957 had caused so much alarm in the US that the event had ignited the space race, with each country striving to outdo the other.

The Kylarn threat was a similar wakeup call and had launched an altogether different sort of space race, in which all the countries of Earth worked together with a common goal.

When they each completed their parts of the check-list, they traded duties for the double-check. JJ moved to the optics, King verified the propulsion systems, and Mira checked the electronics and logic boards. After switching again for one final round, the three Cadets gave the satellite a clean bill of health.

JJ glided to the intercom and transmitted to Central. "Forty-five minutes to spare, Stationmaster. The Eye in the Sky is ready to launch."

Since Tony had already tinkered with robotics and had built devices for science fairs, he was fascinated with the ISSC's robot arm, which would help launch the satel-lite. While JJ, King, and Mira finished the final checklist for the Eye in the Sky, Major Rodgers trained Tony in how to use the system.

The ISSC had four advanced mechanical arms, joint-ed and delicate manipulators that could be guided with absolute precision. The intuitive hand controls made the most advanced videogames Tony had ever played seem like cheap little toys.

One of the articulated arms was connected to the Equipment Module and had specifically been designed to help launch satellites. The plan was to reach in, grasp the Eye in the Sky, lift it carefully out of the open bay, and nudge it off into space, like a gentle slow-motion baseball pitch. Since it was too dangerous to fire rockets so close to the station, the Eye in the Sky would have to be moved a safe distance from the ISSC before its main thruster could ignite. The rocket would carry the satellite far away from Earth to L-4, the gravitational balancing point, where it could keep an eye on the Moon.

"I trained for months on this system," Rodgers said to Tony from a viewscreen on the wall. His skin looked gray and pale, and his hands continued to shake. "But I'm in no condition to launch the satellite—and it needs to go."

"Don't worry, just show me what to do," Tony said.

Rodgers watched him at the controls, instructed him in how to move the mechanical grasping arm up and down, side to side, and in combinations. "It's not complicated, but it might feel unnatural at first."

Tony had used smaller waldoes to pick up weights and samples that were sealed inside containers during the Challenger Center field trip, but he had never expected to be doing this for real.

The arm raised and lowered. The mechanical clamp fingers opened and closed. "Just like an extension of myself," he said. "I feel like I could close my eyes and just touch the tip of my nose."

"I'd rather you didn't," Rodgers said.

Instead, Tony moved the mechanical hand up and down. "There, I'm waving!"

"You seem comfortable enough with the systems, Cadet, but you're not ready yet. I have devised a set of special exercises—tiny manipulations designed to enhance your dexterity with the mechanical arm. I want you to feel like you're able to shuffle and cut a deck of cards in space."

Tony laughed. "All right, then! By the time we're done, I'll be ready to play poker with the Kylarn."

Normally, aboard the space station, Dr. Romero would have little to do in the sickbay—very few crewmembers were ever sick or injured—so her duties included numerous biological experiments as well. Many of the tests were similar to those Song-Ye had helped the doctor conduct on Moonbase Magellan, studying plant growth and the effects of adverse environments on laboratory animals, such as the hamster Newton.

"I've still got patients," Romero told Dyl and Song-Ye, "but some of these experiments need to be checked or the data won't be useful."

"And the mice, rats, and hamsters still need to be fed," Song-Ye said.

"Just don't give them anything with food poisoning in it," Dyl added. They all groaned.

"It would be a big help if you cadets could check the water supply to the plants and animal cages and dispense the proper amount of food." Romero smiled. "Try not to play with the lab animals too much."

Song-Ye was clearly disappointed. "Isn't that part of the experimental requirements?"

"All right—just don't let any of them loose. Nobody wants to chase around a weightless lab rat!"

Small cages of hamsters, white mice, and lab rats floated among the hydroponics globes, surrounded by the fresh-smelling fruits and vegetables, the bubbling of the water-recirculation channels. One of the hamsters tumbled along inside a weightless transparent ball. The creature had been born up here in orbit and had never set foot on solid ground.

"We were trying to get the lab mice to work on tiny treadmills," Romero said, sounding amused, "but that experiment didn't work out as planned."

After consuming plenty of electrolyte fluids and medications, Lifchez and Rodgers were stable enough that Dr. Romero grudgingly let them leave Medical for an hour, although they still looked extremely ill. Queasy and shaky, and in no condition to operate controls, they gathered in Central to observe the deployment of the Eye in the Sky.

"Relax," JJ said to them. "We've got it covered."

A proud JJ, King, and Mira watched as the Equipment Module was depressurized and the bay doors opened. Although Rodgers was still too unsteady to manipulate the controls of the robotic arm, fortunately Tony had passed his training with flying colors, and had mastered the sensitive operations. The payload specialist judged him to be the most skilled, *healthy* member of the crew for the moment, and recommended him to operate the robotic arm. There was no margin for error.

Using delicate adjustments, Tony bent the manipulator arm downward from the exterior of the station, watching the screen and the camera. His eyes were fixed with complete concentration as the multi-axis arm reached into the module like a complicated extension of his own arm. Breathing slowly and carefully, he closed the clamps a few millimeters at a time to grasp the Eye in the Sky. "Got it."

"Ready for deployment," Rodgers said in a wobbly voice. "Use an easy touch, Cadet."

JJ watched closely as Tony gently guided the satellite out of its holding cradle, then drew it out of the ISSC, where it could be released into space. Once the Eye in the Sky drifted far enough away from the space station, a propulsion rocket would push the satellite into a higher orbit and accelerate the automated satellite all the way out to L-4, the stable orbital point. When it reached the Lagrange Point, the Eye in the Sky telescopes would orient themselves to keep watch on the distant Moon. Attitude-control thrusters would keep all of the sensors aligned in the right direction for uninterrupted observation.

"We ran simulations of the propulsion systems again and again, and ran simulations," Lifchez said. "But you never know whether it will work until it actually works."

Pi started the countdown after the satellite reached a safe separation distance from the ISSC, gradually falling behind them in orbit. When the Eye in the Sky was just a small speck, they were ready for positioning. Dr. d'Ameida's external telescopes showed a magnified image of the satellite.

"Use the attitude-control thrusters to align to the precise vector, Mr. Pi," Ansari said. "The satellite has to be pointed in the right direction when the rocket thrusters burn. Once it heads out to L-4, the Eye in the Sky will be out of our reach." The rocket would lift the satellite far away from Earth, out to the distance of the Moon, but well ahead of it in orbit, like the pace car in a race.

"Testing attitude-control number one." Pi fired a short burst of the compressed gas, which set the satellite slowly spinning. "And attitude-control number two." An equal burst in the opposite direction slowed the rotating Eye in the Sky. "Perfect. Now for number three. This one's to put it on the correct trajectory, and then we can ignite the main thruster rocket." He fired a burst, and JJ saw a tiny puff of gas hissing out of the thruster. Telescope images picked up all the details.

Suddenly another bright flash emerged from the first attitude-control thruster, a jet of steam much stronger than the opposite one.

"That's not supposed to happen," JJ said.

"Attitude-control rocket one is still firing," Lifchez said, his voice filled with alarm. "We've got to counteract the motion."

"Then shut down that jet," Ansari said.

But the gas continued to shoot out like the spray from a loose garden hose, making the satellite wobble out of control.

"The shutdown valve isn't responding, Stationmaster!"

Mira hurried over. "We checked all those systems ourselves."

Pi and Ansari both sent command signals to the satellite, but the high-pressure gas still sprayed out from the jammed thruster. The Eye in the Sky was now doing uncontrolled pinwheels in space. JJ groaned out loud.

"Those jets are designed only for delicate alignment," Lifchez said, looking nauseated, but it had nothing to do with his illness. "We've already used up more than a month's worth of fuel! We don't have that much to spare."

JJ, King, and Tony crowded close, although they could do nothing to help. Lifchez tried working the controls himself, but despite using every trick he knew about controlling the satellite, he, too, was unsuccessful.

Major Rodgers said, "Now it's going to take all of our remaining fuel just to stabilize the Eye, and even then I don't know if it'll be enough." The two Sat team members looked at each other in dismay. "We'll have to retrieve the satellite and start all over. It's impossible to make our scheduled launch window."

Finally, the struck thruster ran out of fuel, and Lifchez was able to stop the most severe wobbling. But the satellite was far from the station. "I think it's stable for now, but even if we managed to launch it out to L-4, we couldn't aim it in the direction we need."

"Better cancel the thruster countdown," Ansari said. "We don't want that rocket engine going off unexpectedly."

Lifchez looked gray-skinned and disappointed. "It's our fault," he said with a loud sigh. "We should have been there to run the diagnostics."

Major Rodgers looked directly at JJ, King, and Mira. "We don't blame you, Cadets. We shouldn't have dumped that responsibility on you. We got sick at the worst possible time."

JJ felt a lead weight in her stomach and knew that it *was* partly her fault. She and King had been careful, and had watched Mira work as well. She couldn't understand what had gone wrong. Watching the satellite on the screens, hanging there useless in space, JJ could not drive away her feelings of guilt and disappointment. Earth's best chance to keep an eye on the aliens, was now crippled.

"Normally the space program would have had enough redundancies to deal with a problem like this," Mira said, in a flat clipped voice, "but this was our only shot. The Eye in the Sky is useless."

Stationmaster Ansari did not let the setback defeat her. "It's never our only shot. We'll think of something."

"Someone will just have to go out there and fix the satellite," JJ said, as if the answer were obvious. "And we might as well get started."

FIFTEEN

Like a hovering drill sergeant, Captain Bronsky inspected his new charges. The Equipment Module looked empty without the large satellite inside it.

Dylan looked over at Tony, who seemed excited by the adventure. Despite his amazement, he had adjusted to the fantastic situation and was now determined to help solve the crisis. Dyl noticed that his sister was spending an awful lot of time with him....

For his part, King devoted plenty of attention to Mira. Dyl wasn't sure if King was trying to get more information about the mysterious girl, or if he had actually taken a liking to her. Dyl found Mira a bit too prickly for his taste, although he admitted that Song-Ye wasn't the easiest person to get along with either. Fortunately, Song-Ye seemed more comfortable in weightlessness now.

"If I may have your attention, Cadets," Bronsky said. "This will be a basic training mission so that you understand how to use one of our new spacesuits and how to maneuver outside in space. To assist us in flying over, retrieving, and repairing the Eye in the Sky, you must all be familiar with your suits as well as the Manned Maneuvering Units, or MMUs."

"Cool," Dyl said with a grin. "Spacewalk!"

"They're called extravehicular activities," Mira corrected him. "EVAs."

Song-Ye gave the other girl a thumbs-up, which seemed to surprise and confuse Mira. Dyl recalled Song-Ye mentioning that in some cultures the sign was considered rude, and he stifled a chuckle.

The Russian captain leaned forward with an intent gaze to impress them with the importance of his lecture. "This is very different from walking on the lunar surface. If you let go out here, you keep going. It's a long way to fall. You will orbit Earth for a long time before you eventually drop low enough to burn up in the atmosphere." He smiled, showing big square teeth. "But you will run out of air well before you burn up like a human shooting star."

"We're ready to learn, sir," said King.

"I'm in," JJ confirmed.

"That's the spirit, Cadets! Normally, all ISSC crew-members would not need spacesuit training. It is a special skill. But with so many of our crew sick, and with the Eye in need of repair, it is best to be prepared."

King nodded seriously. "An Eagle Scout is all about being prepared, although I never got a chance to earn a spacewalking merit badge."

"These suits are large and reinforced," Bronsky continued. "Donning them is similar to how you put on the moon suit. The main difference is the Manned Maneuvering Unit, which has controls and jets to let you move about at greater distances from the station. An MMU allows you and your suit to become a human-sized spacecraft."

"A jetpack!" JJ said. "Let's take it out for a spin."

Knowing what had just happened with the attitude-control thruster on the Eye in the Sky satellite, Dyl said,

"I'm not sure we should trust those little maneuvering jets. What if one gets stuck open? We could be flying off to Venus before we know it."

Mira gave him a scathing look. "You would never have enough fuel to reach Venus."

"It was a joke," Dyl said.

"The cadet has a point," Bronsky said. "That is why we must always—always—keep ourselves connected to the station hull with tethers, until we are ready for longer-range expeditions. Heading out to the satellite will be a major operation, but we will start small. Now cadets, suit up. When you are ready to go, we practice attaching a tether while wearing a spacesuit. After that, we will continue our instruction outside."

Dressed in their bulky suits, they all floated together in the middle of the Equipment Module. Wearing his helmet, the jetpack MMU, and the insulating suit that felt like a sleeping bag with arms and legs, Dylan felt entirely self-contained and isolated. With the helmet radio turned on, though, the others could hear everything he said. So much for whispering jokes to Song-Ye, he thought. Even though he liked to make her laugh, on an open channel everyone on the station would hear his corny comments.

"There are many anchor points on the station," Bronsky said. "Keep yourself securely clipped to one at all times. I've explained the basics of how to use your MMU thrusters, in case you get separated—but don't get separated. If you go drifting out of control, you could knock our communications antennae out of alignment, damage the solar-power arrays, or, in general, make a mess of things."

"We'll be careful," JJ assured him. "Now let's jet."

As usual, Dyl thought, his sister was impatient to try something new—especially if it involved flying.

"Not so quickly, Cadets," Bronsky said. "On your sleeve, a monitor shows your heart rate, oxygen level, and the remaining air in your tanks. Breathe normally. We have plenty of air for a short test mission."

Famous last words, Dyl thought, but decided it was best not to crack a joke about that.

"Now, for basic maneuvering along the outside of the station. Each of you, pick a partner. Your suits have extending tethers, so clip yourselves together. After you anchor one end to the station, one person moves forward and clips the next tether ahead. Always remember, the first team member must not disconnect the anchor tether until the second team member has attached the other one."

"Like a game of crack-the-whip," Dyl said.

"No games, no cracking. This is serious business," the Russian captain said.

Dyl's suit was clipped to Song-Ye's, and she had another long strand in front of her. He bent over and fumbled with his thick gloves to hook his tether to the equipment module wall. Safety first. After checking that each pair was safely connected, Bronsky decompressed the Equipment Module, draining the air into the other station modules, then opened the wide clamshell doors through which the satellite had been launched. Dyl stared out into open space. The starry emptiness seemed to go on forever. "This is awesome."

"Cadets, you may now exit the station," Bronsky said.

The first team members drifted out into space, making their way along the hull of the station, slowly crawling to where they would find a place to clip the next hook. When Song-Ye had anchored them to the outside, Dyl detached the tether inside the equipment module and pushed off, so that he soared out into space. He misjudged the necessary amount of force, though, and went to the end of the tether, pulling Song-Ye along with him until the strand grew tight. That turned out to be a bad idea as they slowly began to rebound.

"Sorry about that," he said. "I feel like a yo-yo." Together, they fell onto the external hull of the equipment module, a little harder than they had planned.

"It takes practice," Bronsky said. "But don't hit any of the equipment. Something the size of a person could cause significant damage."

"As in, don't be a klutz, Junior," Song-Ye said.

Once they moved farther along the space-station complex, Dyl got his first chance to look at the overall structure from the outside. He decided the ISSC was like the framework of a skyscraper under construction. The smooth cylindrical modules were studded with portholes and antennae, diagnostic sensors, and stabilizer jets. The observatory bubble had numerous telescopes and collectors sticking out like insect eyes, as well as large rectangular films used for collecting cosmic rays and solar particles. The giant reflective fan blades of the solar power panels were most prominent, extending out from the main modules, oriented toward the sun.

JJ said, "It looks different from out here. So … majestic."

"The Earth!" Tony cried. "JJ, look at the Earth!"

Below, the blue-green and brown planet looked like an immense whirlpool, frosted with clouds that drifted over the continents. It pulled Dylan's attention like a magnet.

"And look above us," his sister said in a dreamy voice. "Moon, sweet Moon."

"Is there any concern that we might get hit by a piece of space debris while we're out here, like the one that punctured Hab 1?" King asked.

"There is always a chance. We try to keep track of known debris, but space is never a completely safe place," Bronsky said. "Also, these suits don't protect you from exposure to radiation nearly as well as the modules do, so we limit the time allowed outside."

The cadets moved along in pairs, clipping one end of the tethers and releasing the other, like mountain climbers attaching safety ropes to a cliffside. With Bronsky leading, they made their way slowly around the station complex, past the unused hatches on the node rooms that linked each module, getting themselves familiar with the process.

"We will practice these simple exercises first," Bronsky said. Although every movement, every step, required care and concentration, Dyl found it far easier than walking with his crutches on Earth. "The Manned Maneuvering Units are complicated, and we normally don't need them for an EVA, but we will require them when we travel out to the drifting satellite. It is the only way we can repair the Eye in the Sky."

"Someone's got to do it," JJ said. "So it might as well be us."

"No, Cadet. You are not ready, I'm afraid." Bronsky's voice was no-nonsense.

"Let's practice a little more first," Tony said.

The group proceeded to Central's observation windows. Dyl insisted on looking inside, waving at Stationmaster Ansari and Pi, who didn't notice them, apparently deep in consultation with CMC on Earth. The Sat team members, though still recovering in Medical, were busily working out a plan to retrieve and repair the wayward satellite.

Even though the ISSC framework was beneath him, providing an anchor point, Dyl felt awed by the immensity of the universe above him. So many stars and nebulae out there, so many planets, and probably many other intelligent races.

Some of which were enemies, like the Kylarn.

"I'm very … dizzy," Song-Ye said over the suit radio. "Every direction I look, I feel like I'm falling."

Before Dyl managed to connect his end, she fumbled with the connection of her anchor tether and scrabbled with her gloved hands, trying to catch hold of the station, but she came loose. As she flailed for something to hold onto, she only managed to knock herself farther away, while bumping a thin antenna loose as well. Song-Ye floated off, heading toward one of the big, mirrored panels of the solar-power collectors, while Dyl was still a handsbreadth away from his own anchor point. So close … and yet he was unable to reach it! He tried to move, but Song-Ye continued to drift outward, and when her tether stretched taut, she yanked him along with her. They were both going to crash into the delicate solar collectors.

"We're loose!" Dyl called into the suit radio. "A little help here?" He flew past Mira, who extended her arm in alarm to grab him, but missed.

If they struck the solar array, they would cause great damage, maybe even disrupt power to the station … and without enough power, the ISSC couldn't run its experiments, its life-support, its communications. But if they *didn't* hit the array, they would go drifting out to … nowhere!

"Use the MMU," JJ called.

Close to panic, Dyl tried the controls of the Manned Maneuvering Unit. With a tiny puff of his suitpack thrusters, just as Bronsky had showed them, he halted their outward movement and yanked them in the opposite direction, so they began to drift back toward the ISSC—and away from the array.

"Excellent, Cadet Wren," Bronsky said over the radio, sounding very tense. "You did exactly the right thing. No need for another burst. That should be enough."

Dyl was drifting back toward the station, though he and Song-Ye were still reeling out of control, but in slow motion. Finally, a hand caught his and pulled him against the nearest module. It was Tony. Dyl clipped his tether back onto one of the anchor points, and with a light tug on Song-Ye's tether rope, he brought her tumbling back toward him, and caught her before she could strike the hull hard.

"Piece of cake!" he said.

"Maybe *you* should have been a gymnast," Tony said. They all started laughing with relief.

"This was an excellent first lesson, but perhaps we should call it a day," Bronsky said. He sounded shaken by the close call. "I want to see how our colleagues have mapped out the satellite-repair mission, so we know the exact parameters."

Stationmaster Ansari broke in over their suit radios. "Captain Bronsky, this is an alert. Get everyone into the station immediately. We've detected two Kylarn starfish ships heading our way—fast! They'll arrive within minutes."

Dyl turned frantically from side to side, looking through his faceplate. At first all he could see around him was an ocean of stars, countless bright pinpricks, the planet Earth below them—then two bright streaks racing toward the ISSC. *Alien ships*.

He swallowed hard. "We're sitting ducks out here."

SIXTEEN

Bulky space suits were not designed for hurried movement—JJ discovered that quickly enough. While Captain Bronsky was training them, the Star Challengers had moved along the support struts of the ISSC, climbed carefully across the connected modules, and maneuvered their way around the station. But now the group tried to hurry back to the open bay doors of the equipment module without panicking or making any mistakes. They could have cycled through any of the external airlocks in the node rooms, but that would have taken longer.

"Maintain a balance between safety and urgency," Bronsky said. "But please move with all due dispatch."

Song-Ye's mishap had reminded JJ and her friends that one slip could send them tumbling off into space. Drifting out of control would be just as deadly as being blasted by alien invaders. And yet the whirling starfish vessels were on their way, streaking directly toward the space-station complex. They had already seen the Kylarn ships hunt down and destroy the *Recon-1* probe....

On their suit radios, Stationmaster Ansari said, "We anticipate the alien ships will arrive within fifteen minutes. You have that long to get to safety."

"We have to assume they're not coming for a picnic," King said.

"Thanks—we were already nervous enough," Dyl added.

JJ realized she was gasping for breath. The sound of her breathing echoed in her helmet, and the pressurized air tasted metallic. They hauled themselves hand-over-hand along the modules, crossing the gaps between them. Connected by the tethers, the spacesuited cadets played a dangerous game of leapfrog.

The darkness of space with its field of stars was disorienting, and JJ looked in all directions, trying to find where the whirling Kylarn vessels would come from. It was easy to lose track of direction. She oriented herself by the colorful sphere of the Earth below, and the bright Moon shining up above and to her left. Two white lights streaked toward the station—the alien ships closing in.

"After what those creatures did to Moonbase Magellan," JJ said, "I'm not sure we'll be safe even inside the ISSC."

They finally reached the open doors of the Equipment Module. The lights of the approaching alien ships came closer. "It is our best bet for now," Ansari said over the suit radio. "We don't have any underground bunkers to hide in."

Bronsky nudged King and Mira. "Inside, hurry!" Dyl and Song-Ye drifted in after them, tumbling out of control.

Tony bumped into one of the struts, rebounded away, and began to spin. JJ grabbed his arm to steady him, but they both began spinning slowly; however, she stopped their motion with a gentle tug on the tether, then pulled them both back toward the open bay. "I've never done emergency gymnastics before," Tony said. He caught the edge of the bay door and eased the two of them inside.

Bronsky nudged him farther into the module and followed them inside. The Russian captain used a jet from his maneuvering pack to reach the internal controls, pressing buttons with his gloved fingers. The clam-shell doors silently closed, sealing them inside the space station. The chamber began to pressurize, air hissing in with such velocity that JJ could hear the faint echo through her helmet.

As soon as the lights winked green, Bronsky lifted his faceplate and shouted into the intercom, "Stationmaster, we are inside."

JJ and Tony scrambled to help each other remove their helmets, then disconnect the bulky MMU packs. "Maybe we should just keep our suits on," Dylan muttered. "One blast from those aliens could depressurize a whole module—and that's a heck of a lot worse than getting hit with a little piece of space junk."

"What is the status on the aliens?" Bronsky asked over the intercom.

"They have … arrived," Security Chief Napali answered. "But the Kylarn aren't headed toward the space station—they're homing in on the Eye in the Sky!"

"Why would they care about a useless satellite?" King asked.

Mira had also removed her helmet. Her face wore a serious frown. "The Eye is not functional. The Kylarn should have no interest in it whatsoever."

"Maybe they're convinced we can fix it," JJ said. "*I* certainly am … if we get the chance."

With a push against the floorplates, JJ set herself moving toward the opposite wall, where she pressed up against the module's viewing window. She saw two whirligig starfish vessels like the ones that had destroyed the *Recon-1* probe. From a distance, she watched the Kylarn ships slowly circle the observation satellite, as if fascinated. Their movements reminded her of two crows inspecting a squashed squirrel on the road, intrigued and hungry, but cautious, each daring the other one to take the first bite.

"What are they trying to figure out?" King asked.

"Our capabilities," Mira said. "Maybe they're checking it out to see if they need to worry about our space technology."

Stationmaster Ansari said over the intercom, "We're broadcasting this down to CMC. The Kylarn have sent no transmissions, made no attempt to contact us."

"They're not the talkative type," Dyl said.

Suddenly, like birds startled by a passing truck, the starfish ships withdrew to take up a position above the Eye in the Sky. They circled, then turned their pointed arms toward the satellite. Two blazing energy beams struck the Eye in the Sky and obliterated it in a white flash, leaving behind an expanding cloud of reflective debris and the last wisps of propellant gas.

The cadets let out a simultaneous cry of dismay.

"I guess the repair mission is off," Song-Ye said.

"The satellite wasn't functional, anyway," Mira pointed out. "We didn't really lose anything."

"We lost the opportunity to *fix* it," King said. "We could have done it."

Dyl said, "That little demonstration was just for anyone who hadn't yet figured out the Kylarn are the bad guys."

JJ nudged herself away from the window. "Let's get out of these suits. I want to be up in Central."

Working together, they shucked the suits off. Despite their sense of urgency, Captain Bronsky would not let them cut corners. "I know there is a rush, but this is not your bedroom at home. Suits need to be stowed. No telling when we will need to use them again in an emergency."

"As in, *another* emergency," Song-Ye said.

"Remember the moonbase?" Dyl said. "There's *always* another emergency."

Tony let go of his helmet, and it drifted away from him, twirling through the air with the leftover momentum from his rushed movements. Before it could strike Mira in the head, JJ snagged the helmet. "Always secure the pieces. Loose items can cause a lot of damage in zero-G." She still had painful memories of how the pubs bag had knocked her nearly unconscious during her recent training flight with Uncle Buzz; in fact, she could still smell the acrid odor of the smelling salts he had waved under her nose to wake her up.

Mira shot a sharp look at Tony. She still seemed suspicious of how he had so conveniently joined the Star Challengers. "No need to be careless. The Kylarn pose enough dangers without you adding to our problems."

"Sorry." He sounded sheepish.

"No harm done," JJ said. "Let's move."

Working their way through the hatch of the node room, into the next module, and up through another intersection and across, they made their way to the command center. When they drifted into Central, Stationmaster Ansari was floating beside her station with a grave expression on her face.

"What is the status, Stationmaster?" Bronsky asked.

Ansari did not take her eyes off the screens. "After they destroyed the Eye in the Sky, one of the alien ships flew away, but the other one is coming straight toward the ISSC."

On the screen, JJ watched the silvery star spinning toward the space station complex. She remembered what Commander Zota had told them, how the aliens had captured the defenseless ISSC in *his* future, and how they had used the platform to stage their invasion.

"Do you think it's going to blast us, like it destroyed the satellite?" Tony asked.

Song-Ye paled. "Is there any chance we can evacuate?"

"We have two emergency evac lifeboats," Napali said.

Mr. Pi answered, "But we can't get everyone there before that alien ship closes the distance. There's still prep time."

"Even if we launched the lifeboats," King pointed out, "what's to stop the Kylarn ship from just coming after us and shooting us down anyway?"

"I'm not leaving my station," Ansari said, putting an end to the discussion.

"Can the Kylarn get aboard?" JJ asked. "What if they want to capture the station for their own reasons, not just destroy it?"

Captain Bronsky gave a gruff, angry answer. "The ISSC would be a valuable strategic asset—a much closer base to stage an attack on Earth. We must not let them take it."

"I don't intend to," Ansari said.

"They shouldn't be able to get inside," Napali said.

"All node rooms have auxiliary hatches to the outside—it's how the ISSC was constructed, for expansion and flexibility," Pi pointed out. "But it's extremely unlikely that Kylarn hatches would be compatible with ours. How could they dock?"

The ominous starfish ship cruised over the station, analyzing the modules and structure. It circled the ISSC several times, like a prowler searching for an unlocked door.

"They're obviously spying on us," Tony said.

"That goes both ways," King answered. "The station's sensors are capturing images of the alien ship and transmitting them to Earth."

"Maybe it'll just fly away like the other ship did," Mira suggested.

"Good luck with that," Dyl said.

Colonel Fox's voice from Earth crackled through the loudspeakers, startling them. "If we could do anything to help from down here, we would try it, Stationmaster—you know that."

"We're keeping our fingers crossed, Colonel," she said. "We don't know yet what the Kylarn ship wants."

Suddenly, the starfish vessel stopped spinning and approached the node room that connected Hab 2 and the Chemistry and Materials Sciences module. It lowered itself toward the airlock hatch.

"How does it think it's going to get in?" JJ asked.

"I have a feeling they've got a plan," King said.

Then, as she watched, JJ realized just how *alien* the Kylarn race was.

From the bottom of the starfish-ship's body, a ring of pliable metal extruded like soft squishy lips, closing around the external hatch and sealing in a bizarre alien kiss. The metal lips sloshed and shifted, like jelly, until they matched up with the node-room's airlock seals, aligning with the shape. Then the alien metal hardened.

Pi looked down at his controls. He swallowed nervously. "They've made a solid seal with the hatch. The Kylarn are going to enter the station."

Mira spoke in an awed whisper, "Our first face-to-face encounter with the aliens."

"Not ours. I wasn't too crazy about the last time we ran into them," JJ said.

Dyl shuddered. "I have a feeling this is going to be a lot more up-close and personal."

Napali was already moving out of the module.

Ansari said, "I'm not giving up the ISSC without a fight. Come on!"

"We're in," JJ said.

"Right behind you," King added.

SEVENTEEN

Stationmaster Ansari activated a general alarm. "Attention, the ISSC is about to be boarded by the Kylarn! Since these creatures destroyed Moonbase Magellan, *Recon-1*, and the Eye in the Sky satellite, we must assume their attentions are hostile. Security Chief Napali will employ full defensive measures."

"Shields at maximum," Dyl muttered.

"I'm sealing off the Med Module," Dr. Romero reported over the intercom. "My patients still aren't recovered, but they'll fight tooth-and-nail if they have to."

"I'd rather they didn't have to," Ansari said, "but there might not be any way around it."

JJ took the lead as they shot like human torpedoes through hatches, touching handholds to adjust their courses, pulling themselves up through node rooms and intersections, moving toward the CMS module, near which the starfish ship had docked.

Pi received a message as he rushed along beside them. "Dr. Kloor reports that Hab 2 is evacuated."

"It might be a good idea to prep those evacuation lifeboats just in case," King suggested. "Remember, if we hadn't been ready at Moonbase Magellan, nobody would have survived."

The Stationmaster obviously didn't want to give up. "I'll consider that, but I'm not leaving the ISSC unless we have absolutely no choice. First let's see what the aliens intend to do. Maybe we can stop them from coming inside."

Mira warned, "We've witnessed how much destructive power they have. Fighting the Kylarn will harm us more than it hurts them."

The remaining members of the space station crew began to converge from other modules. Pi made an uneasy suggestion, "Maybe we could try to communicate with them, find out what they want. There's got to be common ground somewhere."

"They've already proved they're not interested in peace talks," Song-Ye said.

"We've tried playing nice," Dyl said. "I'd rather kick their butts ... or, er, their rear tentacle cluster—whatever the appropriate body part is."

King was more pragmatic. "Offering them milk and cookies and a chat won't help, but we *should* study them. If we capture the aliens, we can learn about their biology, their civilization—and their weaknesses. That's a lot more useful than the snapshots we got from *Recon-1*."

Tony agreed. "Or, if we could study that starfish ship docked to the node airlock, Earth might be able to come up with a defense. Build on their technology."

JJ considered the idea of getting into that pointed alien ship, testing the controls, taking it out for a spin. She loved her flying lessons with Uncle Buzz. An alien ship would be even more exciting. "Sounds good to me." Commander Zota himself had used stolen Kylarn technology to travel back in time and find the Star Challengers. Having more alien equipment to study could only help.

Security Chief Napali, who had zoomed ahead, re-joined them. Her face looked as ominous as a thunder-cloud. "Not much more we can do to get ready." She brandished a steel pipe as long as her arm, wielding it like a club.

"Don't you have any guns aboard this station?" Tony asked. "Any blasters or laser beams or lightsabers, even?"

"Firing bullets aboard the ISSC would be disaster," Napali said with a frown. "We'd kill ourselves faster than the Kylarn could do it. Projectiles would either rico-chet, or puncture the hull. High-powered lasers would be equally hazardous."

"How about baseball bats? Soft cushions?" Dyl tried. "Maybe harsh language?"

"I've got what I need." Napali smacked the metal pipe against her palm, taking point as they all stopped inside the CMS module.

Because of the experiments and lab tests performed in the Chemistry and Materials Sciences Module, the curved walls held small sealed glovebox chambers, racks of chemical squeeze bottles, computer data stations, and work surfaces. Near each laboratory bench was an as-sortment of tools and measuring instruments connected to retractable thin threads. Many of the items drifted loose on their strings, not clipped back into their proper holders, because the scientists had evacuated their sta-tions in such a rush.

At the far end of the module, Dr. Kloor stood by the sealed hatch to the node room. He turned to look at them, as if he'd been caught doing something he shouldn't. "I heard the ship attach itself," he reported. "I sealed off the node room after I got the other crew out of Hab 2."

"Then even if the aliens make it into the airlock, they'll be trapped in the node room, won't they?" Song-Ye asked.

JJ wasn't convinced. "The Kylarn didn't have much trouble docking to the station. I don't think they'll let a locked door stop them."

Pi came forward, his face worried and pale. "We're going to have to face them, sooner or later."

"I'm not rolling out the welcome mat," Ansari said.

Kloor went to one of the screens at a lab station, toggled through images of various modules on the ISSC, until the screen was filled with gray static. "We have a camera in the node room, but it's not functioning. The aliens must have deactivated it."

At the far end of the module, JJ heard clunking noises from inside the cramped connecting chamber, a thump, then a clang as the aliens emerged from the starfish ship fused to the airlock. Tension hung thick in the air, but JJ pushed aside her fear. She went forward without asking. "Well, somebody's got to see what they're doing."

"Careful, Cadet Wren," Ansari said, but JJ was already moving to the node room.

The indicator lights on the hatch controls flickered, as if the aliens were trying different methods of unlocking it from inside the node room. JJ caught a handhold on the wall and pulled herself toward the hatch.

Behind her, Security Chief Napali stood ready with her club.

JJ maneuvered herself to the small window, getting close enough to see into the sealed room. She pressed her face up against the small porthole.

Suddenly a damp brownish patch of skin flashed in front of her, and then she saw a milky, membrane-covered eye that looked like an undercooked egg glaring out at her. With a yelp, she flinched backward, accidentally let go of the handhold, and tumbled in the opposite direction. Napali caught her, pulled her to safety.

Before JJ could say anything, the Kylarn figured out how to activate the hatch controls. The heavy door unsealed.

"I'm ready with my harsh language," Dyl said nervously. "Who's got the baseball bats?"

The hatch slid open. Moving with freakish speed, two *things* pulled themselves forward in the weightlessness, creatures that were too ugly to stay inside a nightmare. It was as if they boiled out of a shaken soda bottle, racing toward the waiting humans.

The Kylarn were squishy, tentacled sacs, like half-deflated balloons that had sprouted flailing whips. Each alien had two pale eyes and a patchy, vibrating membrane over a soft floppy head. The two creatures lashed out with their tentacles, as if they were lion-tamers' whips, snagging handholds, yanking themselves into the CMS Module.

Napali bravely put herself in front of them, raising the club. "Stop! Leave this station immediately." She faced the invaders, committed now.

The two floating Kylarns hesitated at the security chief's boldness. JJ supposed they must imagine that someone so brave was either powerful or carried a great weapon. How would an alien know anything about human appearances?

The pair of tentacled creatures hung there, waving their whiplike arms for a long tense moment. JJ remembered how they had taken the time to study the Eye in the Sky satellite before acting. Without coming within reach of her club, the Kylarn pointed several tentacles at Napali. Each appendage was capped with a silvery tip that looked like a pointy thimble connected to a thin tube running up the snakelike arm.

When the aliens aimed the thimbles, a murky green substance squirted out that looked like a cross between phlegm and fat noodles. Napali tried to duck sideways, but the sticky strands splattered her, knocking her toward the curved wall of the module and holding her to it, as if she were covered with a wad of fresh chewing gum. The security chief yelped and struggled to pull free, but she and her metal club were glued to the wall.

"Get to safety!" she shouted, squirming in place. "Don't worry about me—fall back."

As the other crewmembers yelled, scrambling for some way to defend against the alien creatures, JJ reached for the nearest screened-off chemical locker. She grabbed a squeeze bottle of scarlet liquid. She didn't know what it was, hoped it might be dangerous. After all, nobody knew what could harm the Kylarn.

The two aliens raced toward the crew, but JJ squeezed her chemical bottle as hard as she could. She squirted a jet of the bright red fluid, and it splattered the soft head sack of the foremost Kylarn, leaving a bright scarlet stain. "Take that, squidbutt!"

The creatures snapped their tentacles like whips and let out an ominous thrumming sound.

Under his breath, Dyl said, "*Squidbutt*—I like that!"

"Retreat!" Tony shouted. "JJ, get out of there!"

The creatures kept advancing. As the crew backed away, Kloor said to JJ, "What were you hoping the red dye would do, Cadet Wren?"

"That was just Plan A." JJ flashed him a predatory grin. "We've got plenty of other chemicals to try."

Napali continued to struggle against the gummy substance sticking her to the module wall, but the aliens had already gone past her.

Reaching forward with their tentacles to grab handholds, the two aliens launched themselves toward the humans, and the crew scattered.

EIGHTEEN

While the humans scrambled to get away, instinct took over—but their instincts were designed for a *gravity* environment. In their retreat from the advancing Kylarn, both the ISSC crew and Star Challengers alike went spinning, bumping, and flying out of control.

Napali continued to struggle as the sprayed goo held her fast to the wall, but the aliens no longer seemed interested in the security chief; she was out of the fight. Hooking their tentacles ahead, grabbing onto handholds, the Kylarn reeled themselves forward.

The two creatures focused on JJ, and she threw the dye squeeze bottle at the red-splotched alien. The stained Kylarn batted it away with a tentacle, then aimed its silver thimble weapon at her.

In hurling the chemical bottle with all her might, JJ lost her grip and found herself dangling in midair. The nearest handhold was out of reach, but Tony called to her. "Stretch your hand behind you!"

With the alien's thimble weapon pointed at her, she snagged Tony's hand. He held one of the grips on the wall, and used it as a pivot to give her a short, sharp tug backward. The alien discharged its sticky web. The substance sprayed in the air, missing her and splattered against the racks of chemical vials and squeeze bottles.

JJ flew like the partner of a trapeze artist, and Tony was expert enough to aim her directly through the hatch behind them. As she shot out of the module and into the crowded node room, she felt less like a circus performer than like a bowling ball. She collided with Ansari, Kloor, and Pi in a tangle of arms and legs, not to mention a bunch of fresh bruises. They all fought their way out of the connecting chamber and into Hab 1.

Tony vaulted through the node room and into the hab module with the aliens right on his heels. Captain Bronsky grabbed Tony and hauled him forward, while the second alien fired a short burst from its web-squirter. The gooey splat caught the Russian captain on the arm, pinning his wrist to the hull of the module. Bronsky strained and tugged, but even though the still-soft glob stretched, he could not break free. The creature didn't fire another squirt at him.

King grabbed Bronsky's hand and planted both of his feet against the bulkhead so he could add extra strength. "This ... *elastosnot* stuff has got to break!" He strained, with the Russian pilot helping, and finally the sticky substance snapped just as the aliens came after them.

King and Bronsky raced off, bringing up the rear, and one of the Kylarn tentacles snagged King's left ankle in a tight grip. Grabbing onto a handbar on the wall, he yanked with all his strength. He dragged the weightless alien through the hatch and flung it like a flailing spider against the opposite wall. The impact made a wet sound, and its brown head sack squished flat. The milky eyes bulged out in surprise. Twitching feebly, the Kylarn spurted its thimble weapon, but the globs of adhesive struck only the empty walls, gumming up one of the open sleep stations. King pulled his leg free of the limp tentacle, and Bronsky hurried him along.

By then, the others had spread out through the hab module and split up, escaping into the connecting passages. Mira led the retreat through the next node room, heading in the direction of the observatory, the Mess Module—and after that, Central. King went with Bronsky, following several crew and Stationmaster Ansari.

Dyl and Song-Ye bolted for the greenhouse and biosciences lab, with JJ and Tony close behind them. The other ISSC crewmembers headed off in other directions.

Tony said, panting, "Boy, when we first got here, I thought this space station was huge, but this wild chase from module to module is making me think the ISSC is way too small. How long before we get cornered?"

"Only so many places we can run from module to module," JJ said.

The two Kylarn piled into the node room. The red-stained alien followed JJ through one hatch, while the other alien, looking equally annoyed, raced through a different hatch.

"If the Kylarn reach the command center, who knows what they can do to the systems? They could destroy the station, cut off life-support." JJ looked back, but they were cut off from Central right now. She knew from Commander Zota's grim stories that these aliens wanted to capture the space station.

"King, Mira, and Stationmaster Ansari can take care of that. We've got other things to worry about," Dyl said.

"If we circle back around, we can help Chief Napali," Song-Ye suggested as they drifted into the large greenhouse. "I don't think she's hurt, just trapped by elastos-not—and we need her."

"Good idea," Tony said. "Maybe we can find some acid or poison in the CMS lab to use against them. Who knows what chemicals these things might react to?"

"I don't think that one liked the new tattoo you gave it, JJ," Dyl said, pointing back the way they had come. "Maybe the other aliens will call it Red Spot from now on."

The pursuing Kylarn entered the greenhouse module, and JJ had to admit that the bright-red splotch across its "face" was quite impressive. She couldn't tell whether the blobby thing looked angry or not.

The greenhouse module dead-ended, and they had no place to go. Whipping its tentacles forward, the Kylarn grasped the globes of plants for tentacle holds, damaging them in the process.

"Now might be a good time to try your harsh language on them, Junior," Song-Ye said.

The young man screwed up his face and yelled. "You sure are *ugly*, Squidbutt!"

The Kylarn flapped its tentacles but did not pause as it came toward them.

"I don't think you scared it," Tony said.

"And I'm fresh out of baseball bats," Dyl added.

With a strange, burbling sound, the alien launched itself toward the four.

The ISSC crewmembers scattered from the oncoming tentacled creatures, rushing into the node rooms and dispersing along the passageways. When the red-stained alien followed JJ and her companions into the greenhouse module, the second creature—the brown, blobby one—passed through another connector, as if searching for something.

King, Ansari, and Bronsky ducked into the fitness module to make a stand. With all the training equipment there, King thought that maybe the three of them could detach the colbert magnetic treadmill and hurl it at the Kylarn.

The alien stopped at the hatch of the exercise module, glowered at them with its sickly pale eyes and fired a long shot of its snotlike goo at them. King ducked behind the colbert, and the spray gummed up the works. Bronsky and Ansari looked for some way to fight back … but the alien paused for only a moment to stare at them, then dismissed the three crewmembers as if they were insignificant. Intent on something else entirely, Brown Blob scurried away from the exercise module and, in a tangle of tentacles, shot up through the node room, into the Mess Module, where it began to clatter and ransack, throwing prepackaged meals around, smashing some of the galley equipment.

King yanked off a few gummy strands of the elastosnot that had sprayed onto his shoulder.

"Where is it going? What does it want?" Bronsky said.

"We've got to stop it somehow," Ansari said, and the three of them emerged from the fitness module, racing after Brown Blob just in time to see it disappear into the next node room, turn left and up.

King suddenly knew: "It's heading for Central! It wants to get to our control center." He kicked off hard from the station wall, sailing past the stationmaster and the Russian pilot. After what Commander Zota had told them, he had no doubts about why the Kylarn wanted the International Space Station Complex.

The three of them burst into Central and found that Mr. Pi was there ahead of them and was already cornered. Brown Blob loomed above the various control panels and display screens—clearly up to no good. Its tentacles reached out in all directions, tapping input pads, scanning the screens with its lamplike eyes.

"Stationmaster!" Pi yelled. "Watch out!"

One of the Kylarn's tentacles thrashed back and wrapped itself around Ansari's wrist, snagging her. She tried to yank her hand away, but the snakelike strand squeezed tighter, pulling her arm.

Another tentacle slashed past Mr. Pi, who ducked. "It's shutting down the life-support systems," he yelled. On cue, alarms began to sound, and the lights flickered in the station.

While Ansari struggled to break free, King shouted to Bronsky. "Captain, let's get that thing away from the control systems."

"That is either very brave, or very foolish, my friend," the Russian pilot said, with a grin.

Acting together, the two of them dove toward the creature, grabbing its flailing tentacles, and began to pull, stretching the Kylarn in opposite directions. The thing squirmed and flexed, but for a few moments at least they dragged it away from the station controls.

Pi knew exactly what to do. He jumped back to one of the terminals and reset the systems, activating life-support and closing the valves that bled oxygen off into space.

As King and Bronsky struggled with the tentacles, and Ansari broke herself free, King realized that the two Kylarn intended to make the station uninhabitable, to kill and discard all the crewmembers. Then the aliens could take the ISSC for themselves. He didn't intend to let that happen.

Using moves he had learned from his kickboxing training, he attacked Brown Blob. The alien, surprised by their desperate resistance, turned its attention from the station controls again. Thrashing, the alien wrapped one tentacle around King's waist and grabbed Bronsky by the throat with another. Then it began to squeeze.

NINETEEN

JJ's eyebrows drew together as Red Spot closed in on them in the greenhouse module. "Since Commander Zota told us to do personal training, I've got some pretty strong muscles. With a little help from you"—she looked over at Tony—"I could become quite a projectile."

"You got it! Crack-the-whip, zero-G gymnastics … just an average day of alien fighting."

"I'll kick off from the wall. Tony, take both of my hands and swing me as hard as you can to add momentum. I'll keep my legs straight, and as long as you aim right, I'll plow right into that thing."

Red Spot lurched toward them, looking ominous. Tony hooked his feet through one of the handhold rungs. He took JJ's arms as she bent backward, counting, "One—two—*three!*" She launched herself, and Tony flung her like a discus.

JJ shot feet-first through the air. She stretched out her legs, leading with her heels. Ten feet from the attacking alien, she thought, *I sure hope that thing doesn't pop. Eww.*

She plowed into the soft and sagging bag that was its head. Her feet sank into it up to her ankles, and Red Spot's bulbous sac collapsed as if it were a jellyfish. What if it swallowed her?

The rebounding Kylarn struck the greenhouse wall, clattering bean and tomato plants out of the way. When it hit the side of the module, Red Spot recoiled and pushed off with its tentacles. The alien flew across the greenhouse—straight toward Song-Ye and Dyl. Thrumming and shuddering, the creature pointed its silver thimble and squirted a mass of goo that drenched Song-Ye like a bucket of runny sealant.

She cried out in disgust and fear. "The elastosnot got me!"

"I'll keep it away." Instinctively, Dyl grabbed for anything nearby—a small fire-extinguisher canister. As Red Spot approached Song-Ye, looking enraged now, Dyl sprayed a blast of white vapor.

Struck by the fire-extinguisher jet, the Kylarn reacted much more frantically than when JJ had squirted it with scarlet dye. Red Spot writhed as if it had been hit with bug spray, crumpling, reaching backward with a tentacle to grab onto anything to pull it away.

"Don't like that, huh?" Dyl shouted. "I'm having a blast—how about another one!" He fired a long burst from the fire extinguisher, and the jet sent him spinning backward.

JJ had caught herself on the other side of the module, panting. For a split second, the whole scene went into slow motion before her. Dyl was using a fire extinguisher to battle the Kylarn intruder. Since their father had died in a burning house, JJ's only phobia had been fire. The Kylarn were an immediate danger, though, and Dyl was fighting them just like he would fight a fire. Genius! Dad would have approved.

Tony scrambled after her. There was a second canister nearby, and she yanked it from its hook on the wall. So as not to be knocked backward, she held on and directed a long blast at Red Spot. "Back off, Spot!" The alien was in full retreat now, and JJ chased after it.

Tony kicked himself over to the intercom station on the wall. "Everyone, use the fire extinguishers! The squidbutts hate fire extinguishers!"

A burst of chatter came over the station speakers; they could hear sounds of a scuffle, then Mr. Pi's gasping voice. "Acknowledged! The other creature is up here in Central."

King's voice called out, and the struggle continued; a loud, hissing sound from the speakers must have been another fire-extinguisher blast. "Get your squid butt off this station, Brown Blob! Hah! There it goes!"

Glaring at the miserable, red-stained creature that wriggled and lurched its way out of the greenhouse module, JJ knew the tables were turned and both of the aliens were fleeing. She called out, "I'll herd this one back toward the Mess. Let's try to seal it in one of the node rooms!"

While Dylan occupied himself extricating Song-Ye from the adhesive mass, JJ and Tony launched after the fleeing Kylarn. Fortunately, each of the ISSC modules had at least two fire extinguishers for safety, since a fire would be a serious danger aboard the enclosed station. JJ squirted another burst of fire-suppressant gas at Red Spot. Like a cattle prod, the jet spurred the Kylarn ahead.

At the node-room intersection with the observatory module, Dr. d'Almeida surprised them by popping out in front of the alien; the astronomer sprayed a fire extinguisher in its "face," so that Red Spot recoiled, changed course, and shot through a different airlock.

King and Stationmaster Ansari arrived, chasing the other alien. They shouted to JJ and Tony, "Herd those things to the node room between Med Module and the Mess! Dr. Romero has Medical sealed, so they'll have no place to go."

"Got it," Tony said.

"Just don't let them get back to their ship," JJ said. "They'll escape."

"Protecting the station is our priority," Ansari said.

In her mind, JJ envisioned how all the station's modules fit together, and she drove the fleeing alien in the right direction. Remembering everything that Zota had told them about what these hideous things intended to do to humanity, JJ growled, "Still don't think humans can fight back? Think again."

Tony seized a fire extinguisher from the adjacent module, launched himself from the bulkhead, and shot past them like a cannonball. He slowed himself by the force of the fire extinguisher blast he released, using it like a retro-rocket. The panicked Kylarn scrambled away, while JJ, Tony, and d'Almeida managed to direct it. The creature obviously hadn't expected this furious of a resistance. King and Stationmaster Ansari herded the second alien, with Captain Bronsky yelling loudly in Russian behind them.

The pair of tentacled aliens raced into the node room that dead-ended at the sealed Med Module. As soon as the two aliens were crowded into the chamber, Red Spot and Brown Blob turned about like cornered rats. They lashed out, trying to fight back, but the fire extinguisher spray made their whiplike appendages recoil. JJ and King quickly sealed the outside hatch.

"Believe me, they're bottled up tight," Tony breathed in relief, looking at the sealed hatch.

"Yeah, and no Get Out of Jail Free card," JJ added.

Ansari, breathing hard, looked satisfied. "Excellent work, Cadets. The hatch into Medical was already sealed." Her fingers danced across a keypad on the opposite hatch. "And now they can't open this one, either. Caught like a bug in a bottle."

Dr. Kloor glided into the room and went to the hatch window to peer in at the two aliens.

"What about the other two hatches in the node room?" JJ asked.

"They don't connect anywhere," Bronsky said, "except to open space."

JJ felt good about what they had accomplished.

Panting, King said, "We stopped them for now. Bet they thought we'd be an easy conquest."

"Instead *we* have two captive Kylarn," Dr. Kloor said. "We can study them."

With a jittery stomach, JJ came forward with Tony to look into the observation port. Inside the sealed node room, the two aliens were busy at the controls, frantically trying to escape, but they could not operate the hatches that led into Medical or back out the way they had come.

King started singing "Hotel California" under his breath, the part about checking out but never leaving.

Tony smiled at the lyrics. "Exactly. They understand that they're trapped."

"Let's not get too smug," Kloor said. "Those squid things still destroyed *Recon-1* and the Eye in the Sky."

He was right, of course. Watching the Kylarn, JJ saw Brown Blob focus on the other two sealed hatches—the ones that led into space. "What is it doing?" She began to suspect the worst. "Uh-oh. Stationmaster Ansari, I think they're trying to—"

She heard a hissing echo, then a loud thump. One of the external hatches burst open, dumping the aliens out of the node. In a gush of evacuating air, the two dying and freezing Kylarn thrashed as they were sucked out into the deadly vacuum of space. Red Spot managed to tangle its tentacle on one of the handholds, but its grip soon loosened and it slithered out.

JJ paled. "They're both gone."

TWENTY

They barely had a chance to catch their breath. After the two large creatures were blown out the airlock to drift like big, frozen projectiles, JJ helped the stationmaster take an inventory of the station personnel.

King, Bronsky, Pi, and Ansari all had bruises and welts from their scuffle with Brown Blob.

Tony's eyes shone with pride. "We saved the station."

"For now, at least," King said.

Dr. Romero and the four members of the satellite team were still safely holed up in Medical module. Dr. Kloor went to free Security Chief Napali from where she had been sticky-globbed to the bulkhead in the CMS module; he discovered that a quick burst of super-cold liquid nitrogen froze the elastosnot so that it could easily be shattered. Dr. d'Almeida reported that she had found Mira in the observatory module, and both were returning to the Mess, where they all gathered.

"The squidbutts weren't on the space station long," JJ said. "Can't do us any more harm now that they're dead, but they sure left a big mess behind." They began to retrieve the scattered food packages and clutter that drifted around the community module.

"Definitely a big mess in the Mess," Tony said.

Dyl was still getting Song-Ye loose from the tangle of spiderwebby goo that had trapped her in the greenhouse module. Finally, they both came in, looking a bit worse for wear.

"During the commotion, five of the experimental animals got loose from their cages, so Junior and I had to round them up," Song-Ye said. "Five floating hamsters and mice, trying to scurry in weightlessness, grabbing onto anything they could find, bouncing off walls—it was a bit of a challenge."

Dyl laughed. "I think we should call them animal astronauts."

JJ saw the red welt on the Korean girl's neck. "Are you all right?"

Song-Ye ran her fingers over the mark. "I'm fine now. That stuff may look like snot, but there's nothing funny about it. It burns and tightens up, and it hurts!"

"How did you get her unstuck from the wall, Dyl?" Tony asked.

The young man grinned. "You mean, after I calmed Song-Ye down from her panic?"

The girl scowled at him again. "That was partly your fault, Junior!"

"How did *I* know it was going to snap back?" Dyl asked. "I was trying to save a damsel in distress."

"*Pfft!*" She rolled her eyes. "I hurt all over, and Junior thinks he's a hero."

Mira sailed into the room, accompanied by the astronomer. "You may be sore, but we're lucky the Kylarn didn't want to use their laser shredders on the space station—it would have hurt a lot more, and none of us would be heroes. We'd all be dead."

Dyl snorted. "Well, you're just a big bucket of cheer-up, aren't you?"

"Just being realistic," Mira said defensively.

"But she's making a good point," JJ said. "I don't think the squidbutts were trying to hurt the space station. They wanted to capture it."

"Looks like it," King agreed. "That's why Brown Blob was in Central before we chased it away."

JJ grinned as a thought occurred to her. "We may have lost the two squidbutts out the airlock, but their starfish ship is still docked to the station. We can study it, analyze their systems, figure out their propulsion, even their weapons. It'll be a goldmine."

Bronsky was already smiling at her. "That knowledge might be worth all of these headaches."

Dr. Romero and her patients offered to assist. Lifchez, Rodgers, Kontis, and Kimbrell tried to help with the cleanup, but were soon doubled over in misery and had to be helped back to Medical.

The Stationmaster called for attention. "We have to make a thorough assessment as soon as possible, figure out where we stand. Who knows what other damage the Kylarn did that we don't know about yet?"

JJ realized that it had been quite a rush when the two squidbutts went in separate directions and the crewmembers scattered throughout the ISSC.

"Right, there's no telling what else they might have messed up."

"We know they tried to take over Central and shut down life-support systems," King said.

"So they wanted *us* dead," Tony said

Ansari's eyes were hard. "We need to have a conversation with Colonel Fox at CMC about how to protect this station against further attacks.

"Earth still has a lot of old-style nuclear missiles in various stockpiles, but I don't think they'd be able to hit those fast-moving starfish ships," Napali said.

"There must be another way," Ansari said. "Staying here is dangerous, but if we abandon the station, we'd be handing it over to the aliens, and we would never regain our foothold in space."

Suddenly, the lights in the Mess Module began to flicker. The connecting node room went entirely dark, and several of the status screens on the bulkhead went out, shutting down. "It's life-support again! Our power is failing," Pi said.

Dyl groaned. "That's a problem."

"Some sort of Kylarn sabotage, maybe?" JJ asked.

"I don't know how," King said. "We got Brown Blob out of Central, and Mr. Pi reversed all of the commands."

"Boy," Tony said, running a hand through his light brown hair. "What else can go wrong?"

"I don't think you want to know," JJ said.

Ansari was sweating as she went to one of the few functioning control terminals. She entered commands and studied the screens with a grave look. "The problem isn't a command from Central. Our primary solar-power array has either been damaged or knocked off line."

"How could they do that?" Dyl asked.

But JJ was already headed toward a viewport, through which she peered into space. She looked at the giant, reflector-covered, windmill-shaped apparatus that converted sunlight into electricity, and saw immediately that several of the vanes were bent, and the entire array had been knocked off its framework. Two flattened masses hung from the array like giant bugs splattered on a windshield.

"Another kind of space junk," JJ said in a grim voice. The bodies of the two Kylarn, even in death, had damaged the station, drifting free and smashing into its solar-power array.

"If we don't get that fixed," Stationmaster Ansari said, "the ISSC can't survive."

TWENTY-ONE

"Good thing we trained for outside activity. This sure wasn't anything we could have predicted," JJ said. By now, she and her friends were supposed to have taken the MMUs over to repair the Eye in the Sky satellite; that, however, was no longer a possibility, thanks to the destructive Kylarn.

Captain Bronsky led the Star Challengers outside on the repair mission. Kontis and Kimbrell had offered to return to duty, but Ansari had refused. "Not necessary—we have a qualified crew, and you're still sick."

The Stationmaster divided the healthy crew into small teams and assigned each a responsibility. The teams were combing over the station modules to repair any damage the Kylarn had done. Mira had volunteered to clean the hardened alien adhesive off of the walls, collecting samples so that chemists could study it.

At the same time, the EVA crew had to make emergency repairs to the solar panels so the station could get back to normal.

JJ thought of how the Star Challengers had gone out from Moonbase Magellan to erect new solar-power arrays … which the Kylarn had also destroyed. Every task out in space was complicated—moving in a bulky suit, using clumsy gloves, and manipulating tools in microgravity—but *somebody* had to do the work, and it might as well be the Star Challengers. Captain Bronsky would guide them.

"This has *not* been a good day," Song-Ye muttered, and her voice was transmitted through the helmet radios.

Tony gave a wry response. "That's the result of your thorough analysis? We're alive, and we kicked some alien butt, didn't we?"

JJ reviewed the last few hours in her mind—the arrival of the Kylarn spacecraft, the malicious destruction of the blind Eye in the Sky, the two creatures forcing their way into the ISSC and wreaking havoc before sacrificing themselves out an airlock. To add insult to injury, the drifting alien bodies had damaged two of the primary solar power panels! JJ groaned just to think of it all.

"It'll get better," Dylan said. "We've shown the squid-butts what we're made of. They won't mess with us any-time soon."

"Right," Song-Ye said, "Not for at least ten minutes."

Bronsky and King carefully made their way along the large array of delicate reflector sheets. The two dead Kylarn were there, frozen solid and splayed out … disgusting. "Cadets, help me remove this *debris*," the Russian said. "Attach the alien bodies to tethers. Earth scientists will want to study them, but for now we must get the solar-power panels working."

Dyl and Song-Ye retrieved the hard, monstrous carcasses, clipping tethers to the petrified tentacles and pulling the dead aliens away so that King, Tony, and JJ could help Bronsky lift the solar-power array erect again and reattach the connectors.

Two of the array's shining vanes had been damaged. "They'll have to be replaced, but that is for later," Bronsky said. "For now, we restore the connections so the solar collectors will feed energy into the station. It will keep us alive."

JJ was struck by just how fragile everything was. Though the space program tried to plan for emergencies, to install safety procedures and backup systems, humans on the space station were still pioneers living in an extremely hostile environment. Fortunately, the crew was resourceful and could fix any number of problems with the materials at hand. That's what they were good at.

But no one had planned for an alien invasion.

With the Russian pilot guiding her, JJ made the final connection while King and Tony anchored the support strut for the solar array back onto the ISSC's hull. Ansari's voice came over the helmet radio, sounding overjoyed. "That's partial power restored. You did it, team! Now we have enough to meet our basic requirements."

"Check another emergency off our list," JJ said.

Bronsky rounded them up. "Time to get back inside. We need to contact Collaborative Mission Control and discuss what to do next."

Inside Central, Mr. Pi operated the comm station. "Transmission complete, Stationmaster. I've relayed all the information to CMC. Every little clue helps."

"Those two frozen Kylarn specimens and their intact ship will give our scientists plenty to work with," Dr.

Kloor said. For once he sounded optimistic rather than grumpy.

"Now that we know the trick, maybe we can take a bunch of fire extinguishers and raid the Kylarn base on the far side of the Moon," Dyl suggested.

Security Chief Napali, with few gobs of sticky material still stuck to her hair, looked feisty after her ordeal. "I'll be sure to suggest it during the next Earth Defense Council meeting."

Before any of them could relax for a second, the loudest alarm JJ had heard so far blasted through the speakers. The siren sound was different this time, a grinding klaxon—a new kind of emergency.

"What now?" Song-Ye groaned.

Stationmaster Ansari looked as if someone had dumped hot coffee in her lap. "That's the station evacuation alarm!" She whirled to Pi. "I didn't call for an evacuation."

"It's automated, Stationmaster. Sensors triggered it." He entered commands and searched through menus to find more information.

"Are more Kylarn coming?" Dyl asked.

"Not that I can see." King peered out through Central's observation window.

Dr. Romero's voice spoke over the intercom. "What's the nature of the emergency? Do I need to get my patients ready?"

A chatter of voices came over the speakers, asking what was going on. Ansari looked particularly upset as she peered down at the flashing alerts on the screens. "Oh, no! After all we've been through…"

"It's an ammonia coolant leak," Pi reported, his voice strained. "Our atmosphere is tainted—levels are rising."

"Then we'd better patch the leak," Tony said. "Compared with everything we've done so far, how hard can it be?"

"It's not that simple. We have air-quality monitors throughout the station modules," Bronsky said with a suspicious sniff. "Look at those readings."

"I don't smell anything," Song-Ye said.

"You will soon," Ansari said. "The internal workings of the ISSC are cooled by ammonia—NH3—in external cooling loops. If there's a leak across the cooling loop, then deadly ammonia could get into the water and air of the station. Quantities can ramp up to fatal levels in minutes."

"I'll bet one of the Kylarn did it when they were here," Dyl grumbled. "They were trying to get rid of all humans on the station."

"No choice now," Ansari said, her voice filled with disappointment. "That's one of the only situations in the ops manual that calls for an immediate and complete evacuation."

"Shouldn't we check it out first?" JJ asked. "It could just be a Kylarn trick."

"Look at those readings—it's not a trick," Pi said.

"I wouldn't be surprised if they sabotaged something on their way through the station, but this is one thing I'm not sure we can fix in time," Ansari said. "The regulations are clear. A serious ammonia-coolant leak requires us to abandon the station. With the levels increasing at such a rate, we could all suffocate before long." She looked grim and sickened as she activated the intercom. "Dr. Romero, prepare your patients."

"One thing leads to another," Dyl said, "and each one gets worse."

JJ felt a deep frustration. "After all we worked for, after how hard we defended this place, now we just have to … leave?"

"How long can you hold your breath?" Song-Ye said. "Ammonia is poison—you can't breathe it."

King sniffed the air, perplexed. "But I still don't smell anything."

"By the time you smell it, it's too late," Bronsky said.

JJ winced. "This is exactly what the Kylarn wanted—even if it is a real emergency, we can't just leave the station empty so the squidbutts get their tentacles on it."

Ansari was grim and nodded to Napali. "Security Chief, is there a way to scuttle this station after we leave? I'd rather wreck it than let the aliens have it."

"I'm sure I can rig something, Stationmaster. But we have to authorize it through Colonel Fox."

More lights flashed on the alarm screen, and Pi called out, "There's a second alarm, another set of air-quality monitors registering high concentrations of NH_3!"

JJ remained skeptical. "But how could we possibly spring two leaks at once?"

Pi said, "A leak would normally spread through the ventilation systems."

"But the diagnostics came back clean," King said. "Everything seemed fine."

"The Kylarn," Song-Ye said, as if that explained everything.

"That's it." Ansari clenched her teeth, but she was the Stationmaster, and she knew immediately what she had to do. "Contact the CMC and inform Colonel Fox that we have no choice. Prep both emergency lifeboats. Instruct all crewmembers to report to the nearest lifeboat. Everybody, grab emergency breathing masks."

Dyl pointed out a problem. "Those lifeboats were designed for the crew you have on hand. With the five of us and Mira, can you fit six extra passengers aboard?"

"It'll be crowded, I won't argue that," Ansari said. "We can survive long enough to descend through the atmosphere and splashdown in the ocean. The lifeboats are primitive ships compared with ISSC. We've needed to replace them for a long time, but there were always higher priorities."

"I should go find Mira," King said, troubled.

"She knows how to get to the escape craft, if this is an evacuation alarm," Song-Ye said. "We all got the info."

JJ felt a great sense of loss. "I don't like this one bit."

Pi pointed to the readings on the screens. "You can't argue with the data. Ammonia is rapidly building to lethal levels."

JJ checked the source of the second leak—the Equipment Module? She didn't think the Kylarn had even made it there in their raid on the ISSC. Besides, Dr. Kloor had leak-checked the Equipment Module while the Star Challengers were out repairing the solar array.

Stationmaster Ansari activated the station-wide intercom. "Everybody, you know the drill. We have no choice but to abandon the station. All hands, evacuate the ISSC."

TWENTY-TWO

The space station's evacuation lifeboats were outdated craft even older than the supply ship *Halley*, which Bronsky had retooled as the *Recon-1* probe. With Earth scrambling to get its space technology up and running again since the Kylarn attack on the moonbase, there simply hadn't been enough time to design and install sophisticated add-ons. Dylan just hoped the two old ships would hold together long enough for everyone to get safely down to Earth.

He and Song-Ye rushed to the Medical module to help Dr. Romero with the patients. Lifchez, Kimbrell, Kontis, and Rodgers still looked queasy, even after two days of recovering from their illness; the doctor said that food poisoning was rarely so persistent, but they were definitely improving.

"I hope they have air-sickness bags aboard the lifeboats," Lifchez said. "I'll try to hold it in, but no promises."

Dyl didn't want to imagine *that* kind of mess in a crowded lifeboat streaking back down through the atmosphere to the ocean. He said, "Let's bring some supplies just to be safe." Dyl reached into a cupboard and pulled out a handful of barf bags.

Before they headed out, Song-Ye went to a medical cabinet and withdrew oxygen masks, passing them to everyone. Dyl sniffed deeply again. He knew what ammonia smelled like from household cleaning chemicals, and high concentrations would have stung his eyes and burned his nose, but he knew not to argue with safety procedures.

Song-Ye, Dr. Romero, and he helped propel the patients through the Mess Module, past another node room, to the Equipment Module; the first emergency lifeboat was connected just outside. Dyl helped the Sat team members move forward. If they had been under normal gravity, several of them would have been too weak to stay on their feet.

The station lights were flickering everywhere with brownouts from the partially repaired solar-power arrays. Stationmaster Ansari's voice came over the ISSC intercom. "Final evacuation in fifteen minutes. Everybody aboard the lifeboats. Use your oxygen masks in the meantime. Trust me, you don't want to be left behind."

On their way to the evacuation craft, a third air-quality alarm began to sound. Pi's voice sounded surprised. "Strong ammonia concentrations detected in the observatory module—the highest recorded yet. Everyone, get to the lifeboats."

When Dyl and his companions arrived with the patients, King floated in along with Security Chief Napali. The hatch to the old stripped-down lifeboat was already open, and Stationmaster Ansari remained outside the evacuation craft, her face grave, her eyes narrowed with concern. She ushered people inside. "We'll have to crowd together. Pack yourselves in like sardines."

Dr. Kloor was nowhere to be seen, nor was Mira, Captain Bronsky, Mr. Pi—or JJ. Dyl could only assume, and hope, that they were at the other lifeboat.

The timing of it all seemed much too convenient. This whole succession of catastrophes just didn't seem like an accident to JJ.

She knew that in Zota's dark version of the future, the Kylarn had taken over the ISSC, and she had to assume that was what they wanted here and now. But she had expected the aliens to do it by sheer force—not treachery.

The entire Sat team suffering from food poisoning at once, then the malfunction of the Eye in the Sky satellite even after they had checked all the systems so carefully. She couldn't have done anything about the Kylarn scouts trying to take over the station, or the solar array damaged by their own flying bodies ... but everything else made her suspicious. Now an ammonia leak? It was too much to swallow.

When the third air-quality alarm went off in the observatory module, she was convinced.

While it was *possible* the marauding aliens had caused damage as they swept through the station, JJ knew for a fact that neither Red Spot nor Brown Blob had made it all the way up to the astronomy module. Something, or someone, else must have caused that leak. And as she reviewed the crises in her mind, one after another, JJ realized there was one common factor....

Even as the remaining crewmembers rushed past on their way to the second lifeboat, JJ headed in the other direction. Bronsky let out a gruff yell over his shoulder, dismayed to see that she wasn't following. "Only ten minutes, Cadet Wren! We must get to the lifeboat."

"I'll be there, don't worry," she called back. She hadn't seen Tony in some time.

But she wasn't convinced of the emergency. JJ half-expected that this whole evacuation was a trick, and she intended to discover the truth before everyone abandoned Earth's only space station and left it hanging there like ripe fruit for the aliens to pick. And someone seemed to be working with the Kylarn to make trouble for the ISSC.

Commander Zota had sent the Star Challengers into the future to train and to see what lay in store for the human race if her generation's priorities didn't change. Tony had shown up at the Challenger Center at the last minute, completely unprepared for this amazing adventure, but he had seen it all with his own eyes. No one could have any doubt the destructive Kylarn intended to enslave or exterminate all of humankind. It was so obvious! There was no gray area.

JJ raced hand-over-hand, grabbing a rung on the wall and launching herself forward so that she soared through one module, into a node room, and up into the next module. She touched the walls with her hands or feet, guiding herself along. JJ had no time to enjoy the grace of maneuvering without gravity. She had to hurry. The lifeboats were going to launch in only a few minutes—and she either had to be aboard, or else prevent the evacuation entirely.

Breathing hard, she grasped one more handhold and pushed herself up into the dedicated astronomy module. She was disappointed—but not surprised—when she saw who was hunched over the air-quality module tinkering with the sensors.

"I thought it would be you," JJ said.

TWENTY-THREE

Caught red-handed, the culprit looked up from the air-sensor array, but Mira's reaction was not at all what JJ expected to hear.

"Good, you can help me! I think I've already guaranteed the station evacuation, but we can't leave anything to chance. We have to make sure Security Chief Napali can't arrange to scuttle the ISSC before the lifeboats depart."

JJ was taken aback, unable to believe what the other time-transplanted girl was suggesting. "*Help* you?" Though she didn't understand what Mira was doing, or what her motives were, JJ knew she had to stop her.

While the other girl continued to sabotage the sensors in the observatory module, JJ kicked off from the wall and shot toward her like a battering ram. Colliding with Mira, she knocked her away from the air-quality monitor, and they both went tumbling and flailing through the air.

"What are you doing?" Mira yelped, struggling against JJ.

A gauze packet of tiny crystals left the other girl's hand, sprinkling out to float like snowflakes in the air. JJ caught a sharp potent tang of ammonia. "Those are *smelling salts*!"

Mira's kick caught JJ in the stomach, knocking the wind out of her. The girls separated with the force of the blow, flying in opposite directions. Panting, the other girl explained, "Ammonium carbonate crystals—they release NH_3 gas, the easiest way to trigger false emergency readings in the air sensors. Mentor Toowun said it would be a simple and elegant way to evacuate the ISSC without hurting the people or damaging any of the systems."

"You *want* to give the station to the Kylarn?" JJ caught herself on a wall of the module. "You're trying to surrender to the aliens?"

Mira seemed confused by JJ's failure to support her. "Of course! You know what the Kylarn will do if we don't give it over voluntarily. I was sure we all had the same mission. We're here to save lives. Didn't you come from the past? Aren't you preparing, in your own time, for the arrival of the Kylarn?"

"Yes, we're preparing—preparing defenses against them to save the human race. Not to surrender! You're a … a *collaborator* with the aliens! You're on their side!"

"Not at all. I'm on the side of *surviving*. I don't like the Kylarn any more than you do, but it's the only way to save humanity." Mira's hazel eyes were bitter. "Face reality—human science is too far behind, and we can never match Kylarn weapons and technology. Mentor Toowun showed me what will happen if we try to resist. He escaped from that horrible future—he's seen it with his own eyes.

"Humans are going to lose either way, but if we fight back, we only bring more destruction on ourselves. We have to show the Kylarn that we're no threat to them and hope for the best. If humans try to defend against the invasion, they will surely fail and invite retaliation and total disaster." She seemed absolutely sincere.

"But millions will die if we just surrender! How can you allow that?"

"Millions, yes," Mira said. "But if we don't do it, *billions* will be massacred—a hundred times as many people. I'm trying to *save* whole populations. Mentor Toowun came from the future where billions did die, where all of humanity was crushed and broken. I intend to stop that from happening."

A thought occurred to JJ. "Wait—you were working on the final checks for the Eye in the Sky satellite. You sabotaged it, didn't you?"

"Of course. If that spy satellite had been functional, Earth would have been able to launch defenses, and that would have angered the Kylarn. After I added the toxin to the sat team's meals, I thought that the Salmonella would prevent them from completing work on the Eye in the Sky, but you and King ruined that solution. I had to take backup measures again and again. But now I can hand over an empty space station to the Kylarn, and they'll have no need to punish us. It's the best possible solution."

JJ didn't know whether to despise or pity the girl. "That's ridiculous. Those creatures don't think the same way we do. Helping them won't work."

Mira shook her head. "*Fighting* them won't work. If your Commander Zota came from the same future, didn't he say the same thing?"

"Commander Zota believes the disaster can be prevented—if we get our act together and boost Earth's interest in science a generation or two ahead of time. That's why my friends and I have to change the future and fight the Kylarn. We need to be ready."

"You're a naïve little girl," Mira said in disgust. "I can see that I'll have to do this all by myself."

Stationmaster Ansari's voice came over the speakers. "Evacuation lifeboats launch in two minutes! Everyone must be aboard. Cadets Wren, Mira, and Vasquez, you must be aboard—*now*! There is no time to delay."

Red-faced and panting, Tony zoomed into the observatory module. "There you are! What do you two think you're doing? We have to go—now!"

"No, we don't—it's a false alarm," JJ said. "Mira's behind it all."

Tony gawked at the two, then sniffed the air. "Are you crazy? I can smell the ammonia! It must be reaching lethal levels. Come on!"

"It's just smelling salts—she sabotaged the air sensors," JJ said. "She's trying to hand the station over to the Kylarn!"

"Departure in one minute," Ansari's voice said over the speakers. "I hope you three have an alternative way home, just like at Moonbase Magellan."

JJ pushed herself to the intercom and activated it. "Stationmaster, cancel the evacuation! It was a false alarm—sabotage! And we've caught the traitor. It's Mira."

Ansari's voice sounded baffled. "Cancel the evacuation? Cadet Wren, please repeat. Explain yourself."

Tony drifted toward Mira, his expression filled with questions. Before JJ could answer at the intercom, the other girl launched herself off one of the rungs and dove toward the hatch leading out of the observatory module.

Tony moved to intercept her, and they collided in mid-air. He grappled with her, but Mira fought, poked, and scratched like a panicky cat that didn't want to go to the vet. Tony held on, swinging the other girl around, but Mira spread her palm flat and smacked Tony directly on the nose. A spurt of blood came from his nostrils and he let go. Mira planted her feet against his chest and kicked off, driving Tony backward into JJ, then Mira shot through the hatch opening and into the passageway.

Globular red drops drifted in the air, oscillating crimson spheres from Tony's bloody nose. He pressed his sleeve against his face in an attempt to stop the bleeding. "She's getting away!" he shouted.

Though furious, JJ shook her head. "Don't worry, we'll catch her. Where can she go?"

TWENTY-FOUR

Now that her plot was exposed, Mira fled, and the station intercom became a shouting match of confusion and disbelief from the ISSC crewmembers who had been about to launch the lifeboats. Security Chief Napali called for explanations.

Ansari demanded silence from everyone. "I very much want to believe what you're saying, Cadet Wren, but I saw the readings myself, and Pi verified them. Ammonia concentrations are well above maximum. That has to mean a coolant leak."

Tony hung at the hatch, ready to go after Mira, even as he tried to stop his nosebleed, but JJ's priority was to call off the evacuation, no matter what. "Ammonia leaks in three different modules at once, Stationmaster? It was a trick—Mira did it."

"How did she cause the false readings?" Pi asked.

"She dumped old-fashioned smelling salts into the air detectors so that they indicated a lethal ammonia reading. Believe me, it's not a real leak! There's no danger. I beg you—cancel the evacuation. Mira's on the loose."

"We'll find her," Napali said. "Let's break into teams."

"Not so fast. I haven't called off the evacuation yet," Ansari said. "I need proof."

"It makes no sense. Why would the girl do that?" asked Bronsky.

Kimbrell's voice broke in. "We worked with her on the satellite. I thought you were all trying to help."

"I thought she was with your group!" Lifchez said.

"So did we," JJ said. "But we were wrong. She wants the human race to surrender to the aliens. She sabotaged the Eye in the Sky so that Earth couldn't observe the Kylarn activities. She also put something in the Sat team's meals to make them all sick and get them out of the way."

"We *were* all eating with her at the time," Rodgers pointed out.

"We should round up that girl if for no other reason than that," said Kontis.

JJ was exasperated. "Stationmaster, I'm *in* the observatory module right now, the one with the highest ammonia concentration in the air sensors—there is nothing wrong. The air is perfectly fine!"

"I can vouch for that," Tony said, his voice sounding nasal as he pinched the top of his nose. "I'm here, too."

"That's enough for me," Ansari decided. "I hereby cancel the evacuation. Everyone, stand down."

"Stand down? This is no time for a coffee break," Security Chief Napali said. "We've got to stop that girl."

"We know Mira's listening, Stationmaster," JJ said. "But we can come after her from all directions."

"I'll post a guard at each lifeboat," Ansari ordered. "I won't take the chance that she'll slip past us and evacuate on her own. Everybody fan out. Go in pairs if you can. Clear and seal each module, and report."

JJ and Tony warily left the observatory, heading in the direction Mira had fled. When they entered Hab

1, they took the time to open each personal sleep station, just to make sure the girl hadn't hidden in one of them.

"Too bad we can't use a fire extinguisher on her, like we did on those ugly alien critters," Tony grumbled.

"I wouldn't mind giving her a swift kick just for good measure," JJ said. "Mira has been siding *against* Earth, trying to make us lose the war!"

"Equipment module clear," King announced, and then he added in a plaintive tone, "Mira, if you can hear me, please surrender. I know you can hear me. I … thought we were friends."

Silence hung for a few seconds on the intercom. JJ wasn't surprised that the girl didn't answer, and so she said, "Maybe she thought we *were* friends, King. Mira assumed we were on the same side. But she wants to cripple us, leave Earth helpless rather than strong."

"But why would anyone want that?" Dyl sounded incredulous.

"She can explain that after we have her in custody," Stationmaster Ansari said. "We have to find her first."

"Greenhouse module clear," Song-Ye's voice said.

"Mess Module clear," added Dr. Kloor.

"Kimbrell and I are staying in the Equipment Module to make sure she doesn't try to get a suit and go outside," Lieutenant Kontis said. "We don't know how far this conspiracy goes. If she's working for the aliens, maybe she found some way to arrange a pickup."

"Maybe she's going to fly off in the Kylarn ship!" JJ added, her alarm growing. "Better get there and make sure—"

"I already thought of that," Napali's voice replied. "I am at the ship, and I guarantee you she's not getting anywhere near it."

"Biosciences and Fitness are clear," reported d'Almeida and Pi in unison.

"No activity at Lifeboat One," Bronsky said.

"Lifeboat Two is clear," said Rodgers.

JJ and Tony paused to study a station diagram, noting where they and the rest of the crew had searched. JJ and Tony looked at each other. By process of elimination, the answer was clear. "It's got to be the CMS module."

The two pushed forward, swimming through the air like dolphins. They shot through the node room at the same time that King and Ansari converged from another module, followed shortly by Dylan and Song-Ye. Up ahead in Chemistry and Materials Sciences, JJ caught a glimpse of the other girl pulling the mesh off of chemical storage shelves, ransacking the squirt bottles and reading the labels.

"Mira, stop! There's no place to go!" King called out.

The girl whirled in the air, catching herself. She turned to glare at them, looking disappointed—and trapped. A small device with blinking lights was attached to Mira's collar, but JJ didn't recognize it. As the others converged, Mira said, "I'm not worried—I have a ride home. All I need is a smokescreen." She turned, holding a squeeze bottle in each hand like two pistols. Pointing the nozzles at them, she squirted pulsating pools of liquid into the air, one chemical after the other. When the floating liquids collided and mixed in zero-G, they reacted in a boiling thundercloud of fumes and smoke that rapidly filled the CMS Module.

"Looks like Mira studied her chemistry," Dyl said.

"We can't know if that mixture is poisonous or just a nuisance," Ansari said. "We need the air exchangers."

JJ said, "We've still got our oxygen masks from the ammonia alert." She fitted a mask over her face and eyes, while Tony did the same.

During the surprise of the smokescreen, Mira bolted toward the node room. At the far end of the CMS module, the hatch to the connecting chamber sealed shut.

"I have an override," Ansari said. "I can lock her in there, just like we trapped the Kylarn. But what is that device she was wearing?"

"I have no idea. I've never seen one like it," JJ said. Commander Zota certainly hadn't given them anything similar.

Dylan gave his sister a nudge. "Talk some sense into her, JJ. You figured this thing out. Without you, we'd all be evacuating to Earth for no reason, and the Kylarn would have captured the station."

JJ and Tony propelled themselves through the cloying, purplish-green fumes, hoping it wasn't some acid vapor that would eat away at their skin and clothes.

"Keep an eye out for any floating globules," Tony warned. They passed through the smoke screen in moments. "I think we're all right."

Ansari said. "Then the smoke wasn't dangerous. She could just as easily have released sulfuric acid vapor."

"I don't think she's trying to kill us," JJ said. "But she's deluded, and she wants to get away."

Tony said, "Well, we've got her now."

Stationmaster Ansari sealed all the exits.

JJ pulled herself to the sealed hatch, just as when she'd tried to observe the Kylarn emerging from their ship. She didn't expect to see an eye like a milky poached egg this time, unless Mira could somehow change her shape and become one of them. Not a pleasant thought.

"Careful. She might have set up a booby-trap." Tony drifted up next to her while JJ peered cautiously through the porthole into the sealed node room. Ansari opened the hatch.

To their astonishment, the chamber was entirely empty.

After a quick glance through the next porthole, Ansari released the security locks and opened the Med Module—but Mira wasn't there, either. "What happened? How did she escape?" She shot a worried glance at JJ. "There was no alarm, no pressure release. The outer airlock is still sealed, the node room still pressurized. She couldn't have ejected herself to space, like the two aliens did. How could she just disappear?"

JJ shook her head. She couldn't explain to Ansari, but she suddenly understood what must have happened. "If I had to guess, I'd say she's not on the station anymore."

In her mind, she was convinced that Mira had been transported back home, to her own time and her treacherous Mentor Toowun.

TWENTY-FIVE

After the evacuation was cancelled and the station began to recover from the succession of emergencies, Stationmaster Ansari had a long-distance meeting with emergency administrators and Earth's military leaders. Colonel Fox announced an impending launch from Earth so that five additional crewmembers could come aboard the ISSC to help keep it secure. They were bringing components to install a newly designed external defense system in case the Kylarn ships came again.

But it was only a first step; everyone knew that.

Meanwhile, the Star Challengers gathered for a private meeting in Hab 1.

"I feel so stupid!" JJ wanted to kick herself. "Commander Zota warned us about the threat, told us not to trust anyone—how could I not take him seriously?"

"Remember he didn't want me to come along either," Tony pointed out.

"Yeah, that made me think Zota was just going overboard," JJ admitted. "But now I see he was right to be cautious."

"Uh-huh," King said. "I liked Mira, but I guess we were too trusting."

"As in naïve?" Song-Ye said.

"This is definitely a problem," Dyl sighed. They all hung together, comfortable in microgravity now, in front of the empty sleep stations. No one felt like sleeping.

JJ shook her head in frustration. "I *wanted* to trust her! We're facing a gigantic crisis, so it would've been nice to have some help." She bit her lip. "I never guessed somebody would *want* us to lose to the aliens."

"Huh-uh," King said. "What worries me—and maybe I shouldn't even say this—but what if she's right?"

"You mean that we're doomed, and that the human race should just give up before the fighting starts?" Song-Ye asked. "That's not our style."

Dyl blew out a slow, steady breath and said, "But would even surrendering help? I don't see it—those two squid-butts sacrificed themselves to keep from talking to us. If they were willing to negotiate, would they really do that?"

"It wouldn't make sense," JJ agreed.

Song-Ye looked pensive, "Still … they're aliens. Their culture is different. Remember what I said about the thumbs-up sign being rude in some parts of the world? It's a foreign concept. If cultures on Earth are so different from each other, how can we really understand what the *Kylarn*—from a completely different solar system— are thinking? And we don't know what we can accomplish against them."

JJ said, "Commander Zota says the future is our choice. That's got to mean we can *save* people."

King gave a tentative nod. "But what if we make the wrong choices? We're not perfect. We may be able to *go* to the future, but we can't *see* it. We could get someone killed if we don't make the right decisions."

Song-Ye gave an uncomfortable shrug. "And what if Commander Zota is wrong? What if this isn't the way to save humanity?"

"What if we aren't as good as he thinks we are?" Dyl said. "We could make a worse mess of the future than it already is. What if Earth gets blown to smithereens?"

"*Pfft. Smithereens*? Nice word, Junior," Song-Ye teased. "What if we can't do enough to make a difference?"

JJ made an impatient sound. "We could 'what if' until we freeze up and don't try to accomplish anything for fear that we *might* be wrong. That kind of thinking won't help anyone, much less save Earth! It's never a bad idea to get more people interested in science, progress, and leadership. *Someone's* got to take action, so it might as well be us."

King drew a deep calming breath. "All right. So there are a lot of things we know for certain. First of all, *knowledge* is not the enemy. Stupidity is. Ignorance is. If our generation learns science and leadership, looks to the future to understand and to grow strong, then Earth will be much better off."

Tony took up the train of thought. "So Commander Zota is right about having us help our generation learn. Science does a lot of good for the world—cures diseases, feeds the hungry, gives us safe water, puts men on the Moon."

"And women," JJ pointed out.

"Not *yet*," Dyl said.

"Second, we can tell we're doing good work," King continued. "We exposed the alien base on the Moon, and without us, everyone at the moonbase would have died a year ago."

Song-Ye took up the train of thought, "Third, we know the Kylarn aren't peaceful. They didn't come to help Earth. They don't want to be friends, no matter what we do—even Mira admitted that. They're the bad guys, pure and simple."

JJ said, "Then we'll just have to judge the aliens by what we do know. Commander Zota and Mentor Toowun definitely agree on one thing: The Kylarn are going to kill billions of humans in our future."

"The squidbutts didn't exactly roll out the welcome mat the first time we met them on the Moon," Dyl reminded them. "*They* were already sneaking around building a military base. And they shot down the *Halley* just for trying to say hello."

"Not to mention that they blasted an unarmed moon-base"—Song-Ye glanced teasingly at Dyl—"to *smithereens*." Dyl grinned and responded with a teasing thumbs-up.

"The Kylarn don't even want us to have a non-functioning satellite—much less one that might be able to see anything they're doing," Tony pointed out.

King said, "I wish I knew what they were thinking."

Song-Ye said, "We can only look at things from our own point of view, what *we* can see. And as far as we can tell, we haven't done anything to make them attack us. As in, from our point of view, they're jerks."

"*Deadly* jerks," Dyl corrected.

JJ sighed. "We have to go on the assumption, then, that the Kylarn aren't looking for a reason to play nice. Weakening the human race isn't going to save lives."

Stationmaster Ansari chose that moment to enter the Hab module. "I thought it was time I had a private meeting with all of you. After what we've been through together, I think I deserve some answers."

"We've been trying figure out some answers our-selves," JJ said. "Like how we misjudged Mira so badly."

Ansari gave them all a searching look. "I believed that she was here to help, too. You know, Dr. Kloor is convinced that all of you were in on it, as a worst-case scenario ... and as a best-case scenario he believes you're just a magnet for trouble. Who *are* you, and where do you come from?"

Dyl gulped.

"Honestly, ma'am," King said, "we can't tell you. That could mess things up even worse."

"Then how do we know we can trust you?" Ansari looked at them all. She held onto a wall handle, keeping herself steady.

"But we helped save the space station!" JJ objected. "And I'm the one who told you the ammonia emergen-cy was fake. Otherwise you would have evacuated the ISSC, maybe even destroyed it."

"And we helped take care of the patients in Medical and repaired the solar array," Dyl said.

Ansari gave them all a rueful smile. "Oh, I know that. I already used all of those logical arguments on Dr. Kloor. But he's feeling endangered from a source he can't control, so he's reacting emotionally, not logically."

Tony ran a hand through his curly hair. "Boy, it does look pretty bad."

King nodded. "A lot of things have gone wrong both times we were here."

Ansari pressed her fingers to her eyes for a moment, looking completely exhausted. She sighed and looked up again. "I thought we had only the Kylarn to worry about, as if that weren't enough. But now it turns out there are humans trying to sabotage us as well. How do I know whom to trust?"

"We were all sent here by people who think they have the best interests of the human race at heart," JJ said quietly. "Mira couldn't even imagine that I wouldn't agree with her—that the best way to stop the Kylarn is to bow and let them take over. I guess from now on all of us need to be more on guard than ever."

TWENTY-SIX

To make doubly certain that the Kylarn—and Mira—had caused no further sabotage, all of the ISSC's crew, as well as the Star Challengers, combed every module, every laboratory station, every system.

At last, all four members of the satellite team were well enough to return to duty. "Your electrolytes and energy levels are fine now," Dr. Romero said. "There's no need to dispatch you back to Earth for recovery. Clean bill of health."

"I don't ever want to think about getting that sick again," Rodgers said with a long sigh. "There were times I thought I'd never eat anything solid again."

Lifchez commiserated.

King was assigned to the observatory module to help Dr. d'Almeida. Though he tried not to show it, he was devastated by Mira's betrayal. He had been intrigued by the mysterious girl, and excited by the idea of other mentors from the future like Commander Zota. But now the problem seemed even more daunting. How could they prepare for the future?

Now, rather than just being independent, counted on to do what they could, the Star Challengers had to fight against an actual *resistance* group—collaborators with the Kylarn—like Mira and her Mentor Toowun. Their goals were precisely the opposite of Zota's. Mira had fooled him completely, and now King worried about how many others like her might be hidden in society, ready to cause trouble.

Here in the observatory module, he had spent many hours comparing detailed charts of the asteroids that lay between Jupiter and Mars. Mira had actually volunteered to work with him on the assignment. What had she really wanted? Searching for new asteroids had seemed tedious work, less important than the problems closer to home. Why had Mira been so interested?

King found it all deeply troubling.

Dr. d'Almeida was still analyzing *Recon-1*'s images of the secret alien base and how extensive it had grown on the far side of the Moon. Although the astronomer preferred to look at distant galaxies, nebula clouds, even the planets here in Earth's own solar system, she was now completely preoccupied with the Kylarn crisis.

Sure that Mira had been up to something sinister, King was intent on solving the mystery. While studying the stored astronomical images, he attempted to call up the files that he and Mira had worked on, the sky survey charts on which they had identified asteroids.

But the charts were missing, along with King's notes about the newly discovered blips of light. All of their results.

"Dr. d'Almeida, did you move the files of the asteroid maps we compiled?"

"No time to worry about asteroids now, Cadet King." On her screen, the astronomer displayed the images from *Recon-1*, along with the earlier pictures taken of the alien base just after its discovery. She mused, "I'm developing a complete blueprint of the Kylarn outpost, showing how it's grown. I'll also make my best guess as to what all of the structures are for."

"I understand, ma'am, but something's very fishy here. Mira was working on those asteroid maps with me, and now we know that she wants to prevent Earth from defending itself. Why would *she* remove all the charts? She must have had some reason, and I don't think we're going to like it."

Dr. d'Almeida sighed. "How could she possibly care about a set of astronomical maps of asteroids?"

"I'm not sure, ma'am, but she volunteered for that work, and now ... the records are gone. She must have erased them."

D'Almeida came over, leaving the diagram of the Kylarn lunar base projected on the smooth wall. Her brow was furrowed. "But that makes no sense."

"There must be something she doesn't want us to see," King said, then smiled in relief. "Fortunately I transmitted a backup down to Dr. Wu at CMC."

"All right, I'll request the backups from Earth."

"I'd suggest we also retrieve the asteroid maps that Dr. Wu completed at the Moonbase Magellan observatory. His records went back a long time, but I'm guessing we'll find that something important has changed."

The astronomer nodded. "Now that Mira has called our attention to this, I'm very curious to see what it is that she doesn't want us to notice."

Normally, asteroid maps were very low priority, but based on King's alert observations, d'Almeida convinced

Stationmaster Ansari of the potential urgency. All the files were transmitted up to ISSC within the hour, while several teams on Earth also pored over them to spot potential problems.

Once King knew what to look for, an answer jumped out at him immediately. "There's a lot of activity out in the asteroid belt. Look at these images that show white blips, like a swarm of bees—I think that's a flurry of Kylarn ships."

"But what would the aliens be doing out in the asteroid belt?" the astronomer asked, "That's between Mars and Jupiter—nowhere close to Earth. Are they mining for metals? Building more ships?"

"Maybe they're establishing a base out there, like they did on the Moon," King said. "We need to look into this more."

But after he compared the ISSC observations with Dr. Wu's records, using computer comparisons to track any unexpected movements, the answer was plain as day. He suddenly felt cold.

When she saw King's report, the Stationmaster called another emergency all-hands meeting in the Mess. The ISSC crewmembers had just barely survived one disaster after another, and they were all still on edge. JJ, Dyl, Song-Ye, and Tony were also there, just as concerned.

King had transferred the asteroid charts to the main screens in the Mess so that everyone could see for themselves. Ansari nodded to him. "It's your show, Cadet King. Tell us what you've found."

"I don't expect you have good news for once?" Bronsky asked.

"Afraid not, sir." King drew a deep breath.

D'Almeida looked around at the other ISSC crewmembers, who sat at all angles, holding onto handholds. "I assure you all that I have verified this discovery. Cadet King's projections are accurate—and cause for a great deal of concern."

King displayed the asteroid images on the main screen in the Mess Module. He had highlighted the selected dots as he toggled from one deep-space photo to the next.

"In the asteroid field between Mars and Jupiter, you can see some Kylarn activity. The aliens are doing something out there, and you can bet they're up to no good." When he accelerated the sequence of asteroid-field images, three of the bright dots veered off course and began to move along entirely different orbits.

"Every one of these asteroids was in a stable orbit until recently. Comparing the old and new images shows that their orbits have changed—they're on new courses."

Dyl groaned. "Are you saying the squidbutts shoved those asteroids out of orbit?"

"I wouldn't put it past them," Song-Ye said.

"That's what it looks like." King glanced from d'Almeida to Stationmaster Ansari. "Mira purposely deleted these images. She didn't want us to see how the orbits had changed. She was trying to keep us from finding out."

"Why would the Kylarn knock three asteroids loose?" Tony asked.

"They didn't just knock them loose," King said. "Their trajectories aren't random. Those three asteroids were *aimed.*"

"At what?" Pi asked.

"*Earth,*" King said. "They're like giant, slow-moving cannonballs, drawn by the Sun's gravity."

As everyone fell into an angry hush, Dr. d'Almeida called up a diagram that showed the Earth's orbit overlaid with the elongated new orbits of the asteroids. "Look. If you mark out their orbit and Earth's, in less than three years they intersect. Earth will be bombarded by asteroids."

JJ drew a deep breath. "We've got to find some way to stop them. Can't we send ships out to the asteroids and plant bombs, to give them a little nudge out of the way?"

Tony brightened. "She's right! From that far out, it wouldn't have to be much, just enough of an alteration of orbit so that they miss Earth. Space is a big place."

"You don't understand what you're saying, Cadets," Ansari said. "We have less than three years before impact. Earth's space program is just now being ramped up because of the first Kylarn attack. An ambitious mission like that would take far longer. Back in 1961 when President Kennedy called on America to commit itself to put a man on the Moon, the Apollo program was a gigantic project—and it still took almost a decade to accomplish the mission. Earth doesn't have any programs in place that can do something so difficult, so huge, in the next couple of years!"

JJ said exactly what King was thinking. "Somebody's *got* to do it, so you'd better get started."

TWENTY-SEVEN

They had been on the space station for three full days, and all of the Star Challengers were exhausted, physically, mentally, and emotionally. JJ was glad when it finally came time to go to their personal sleep stations for a few hours of rest. She mumbled goodnight to her friends, shut the compartment door, and tethered herself in place.

Only a few seconds after she closed her eyes, she felt something pressing against her back, and her body was saddled with a strange weight. She leaned over to untether herself—or tried to, at any rate, but her muscles barely moved at first. She nudged the wall with her fingers so she could float over and look out the opening of her compartment, but she didn't move. Gradually, the explanation dawned on her, and she knew that the heavy weight all over her body was gravity. They were back on Earth, and she was lying down on something hard and narrow. A bench in the Challenger Center's simulation room.

With considerably more effort than she expected it to take, JJ managed to sit up. In the dim light she saw her friends lying asleep on the floor and benches around her. "Wake up, everyone! We're back!"

"Yes!" Song-Ye blurted out, happy to be on terra firma once more—though she also sounded sad the adventure was over.

"Aw, man," Tony sounded disappointed. "This is it, isn't it? We're back home?"

"You got it—ow," King was also having trouble re-adjusting the effort needed to move, and smacked his hand against the wall as he tried to get to his feet.

"Yeah, back on Earth." Dyl's voice was flat as he awoke with a groan and tried to get to his feet. A pang struck JJ as she once again thought of what returning to full gravity meant to her brother. While for the rest of them microgravity had been a useful novelty, for Dyl it had meant freedom from his uncooperative legs, and now for the second time that freedom had been wrenched from him.

JJ raised her voice. "Commander Zota? Are you there?"

The door opened, and Zota stood in front of them. "Greetings, cadets—and welcome back. Are you ready for your debriefing?" He looked relieved, but tried not to show it.

"I wasn't ready for gravity again, but I'm ready for a briefing," Dyl said with a sigh.

"And do we have a lot to tell you!" JJ said.

When they were all comfortably settled in their mini-Mission Control and briefing room, Commander Zota rubbed his hands briskly together. "Now, tell me, has anything changed in the future?"

King spoke up. "Looks that way, sir. We made a big difference last time. The whole moonbase crew was still alive."

"As in the moonbase was still a pancake, but the people survived," Song-Ye amended. She had already retrieved Newton from his habitat and held the hamster in one hand. The tan rodent's whiskers and nose wriggled with excitement as he explored the new smells on her clothing.

In a rush, their stories overlapping, they described their experiences on the space station, from meeting Mira to the destruction of the Eye in the Sky, to being boarded by the Kylarn, and discovering the oncoming asteroids.

Commander Zota paced the room, listening. "I'm grateful for the progress we made, but most worried about this news of Cadet Mira. I knew of the Kylarn threat ... but not another group that's fighting entirely against what we hope to accomplish. This is very disturbing. Did she tell you the name of this other man from the future?"

"Mentor Toowun," JJ said.

Zota stiffened for a moment, and a dark cloud crossed his face. He sighed. "I know him. He and I both survived the same terrors. For a time we were allies and fought together ... and now it seems we both escaped to the past. I am very disturbed to learn he has taken a different path—perhaps training others, just as I am training you."

"A fifth column?" Song-Ye suggested, with a troubled expression.

Zota nodded gravely. "A very astute observation, Cadet Park."

"What does that mean?" JJ asked, frowning.

King crossed his arms over his chest. "From history, fifth columnists are people who secretly sabotage a group from within—mess things up to help the other side."

"As in, Mira." Song-Ye scowled. "I still can't believe there are humans fighting to *help* aliens attack Earth! If Mentor Toowun saw what the Kylarn did to the human race even before we put up a fight, how can he imagine the same aliens would be merciful?"

"This is definitely a problem," Dyl said.

"I'm afraid we must consider Toowun and Mira traitors to humanity, actively working to help the Kylarn. It is one of the reasons I cautioned you not to share too much about your mission with anyone." Zota glanced meaningfully at Tony. "Are you certain Cadet Vasquez can be a Star Challenger?"

Tony was very earnest. "I'll study whatever I need to and help you spread the word—about science and technology being cool, that is. And I won't say anything about you or time travel, unless you tell me to."

"I trust him—I say he's in." JJ took his hand, smiling at him, then blushed as she realized what she'd done. But he didn't let go of her hand.

"He did pretty well," King agreed. "I think he's a member of the team now."

Song-Ye shrugged. "Whatever, I can put up with him."

"Not a problem," Dyl said. "Just try to remember never to wear a red shirt when we go on a mission."

Tony smiled with relief. "Believe me, I know better. So, do you accept me on the team, Mr. Zota? Can I be a Star Challenger too?"

The Commander pressed his hands together and nodded. "Indeed. So long as you understand that the mission of the Star Challengers is not a hobby, not something you do for a few months or a year and get tired of it, then move on to something else. The aliens coming to Earth are not imaginary. Your mission, all of you, is to help save the world and humankind by becoming tomorrow's scientists, engineers, and leaders. As Star Challengers, you have a great deal of work ahead."

APPENDIX

THE "CHALLENGER 7"

Seven astronauts were lost aboard the final flight of the space shuttle Challenger, STS 51-L, on January 28, 1986. We'd like all readers of *Star Challengers* to get to know them a little better:

Christa McAuliffe was a high-school history teacher from New Hampshire. NASA decided that their first civilian to fly in space would be a teacher, and Christa was selected from 11,000 applicants. A wife and mother with an endearing personality, she was the perfect choice.

Dick Scobee served as the Commander of STS 51-L. Growing up in Washington, he built model airplanes and dreamed of flying them someday. He enlisted in the Air Force and worked as a mechanic on planes until he could go to college and get commissioned as an officer and assigned to fly cargo planes. Later, he was accepted as a test pilot, then an astronaut. In all, Dick Scobee flew over 45 types of aircraft. He traveled with his wife June on field trips with her students and was her best guest speaker. One time, he helped create homemade rockets to teach June's students a physics principle. He also flew in space on Flight STS 41-C.

Judy Resnik served as a Mission Specialist astronaut. Discouraged from studying engineering as a college student because she was a girl, Judy persisted until she earned a PhD as a scientist and engineer. As an astronaut, she helped develop the giant remote-manipulator arm that folded into the cargo bay. In addition she was a classical pianist.

El Onizuka, from Hawaii, served in the Air Force as a test flight engineer and with NASA as a Mission Specialist. His mission on the 51-L flight was to deploy a communication satellite in space. El was an Eagle Scout and supported Scout groups as an adult; he also coached youth softball. He frequently returned to Hawaii to visit schools to encourage students to study and work hard to fulfill their dreams.

Mike Smith was a Naval Test pilot from North Carolina, and assigned as the pilot aboard STS 51-L for his first space flight. When he was a high school student, Mike loved to play football, but often missed receiving a pass on the field because he spent too much time watching planes fly over. He returned to the U.S. Navy Test Pilot School as an instructor and flew 28 different types of civilian and military aircraft. Mike was also a founding board member for the Clear Lake High School soccer team booster club.

Ron McNair from South Carolina graduated from the Massachusetts Institute of Technology with a PhD in physics. On the flight, he served as a Mission Specialist to make crucial observations of Halley's Comet. Ron often made inspirational presentations to schools and colleges. He was a 5th-degree black-belt karate instructor and a performing jazz saxophonist.

Greg Jarvis from California was a payload specialist assigned from Hughes Aircraft to conduct scientific experiments. Always learning and inquisitive, Greg frequently took classes at local colleges—everything from backpacking, to French, to astronomy. After being chosen as payload specialist, he spoke to many elementary schools about satellites and the space program. He was set to receive his Master's in Business Administration from West Coast University while aboard the *Challenger* flight 51-L.

To learn more about all the astronauts who flew space missions on the Shuttle Transport System (STS) flights go to http://www.nasa.gov/mission_pages/shuttle/shuttlemissions/list_main.html (1981-2011)

The Challenger 51-L crew had an official NASA photograph taken, but they also posed for this "unofficial" shot. Though many of their activities would be to conduct scientific experiments in space and launch a satellite, their flight became known as the "Teacher in Space" mission when teacher Christa McAuliffe was assigned to the crew. In this photo, they chose to dress in school clothes, with academic mortar-board caps and school lunch boxes. Front row: El Onizuka, Judy Resnik; back row: Mike Smith, Ron McNair, Christa McAuliff, Barbara Morgan (McAuliff's alternate), and Commander Dick Scobee. (Not pictured, Greg Jarvis.) Photo courtesy NASA

BIOGRAPHIES

REBECCA MOESTA is an award-winning, *New York Times* bestselling young adult author who has written for Star Wars, Buffy the Vampire Slayer, Star Trek, as well as the original trilogy "Crystal Doors," coauthored with Kevin J. Anderson.

KEVIN J. ANDERSON is the #1 international bestselling author of nearly a hundred novels, best known for his Dune novels coauthored with Brian Herbert, his Star Wars or X-Files novels, or his Saga of Seven Suns series.

JUNE SCOBEE RODGERS is a tireless proponent of the space program, June is intent on fostering a new generation of students in science, technology, engineering, and mathematics. Her husband Dick Scobee was the commander on the final flight of the space shuttle Challenger in January 1986. She serves as the Founding Chairman of the Board and as a Founding Director for Challenger Center for Space Science Education. Holding a PhD from Texas A&M University and a Master's from Chapman College, both in Curriculum and Instruction, she has taught in every grade-level classroom from Kindergarten through college. June will oversee the creation of free lesson plans and other materials to support each *Star Challengers* novel, allowing this entertaining series to be used as an engaging teaching tool inside the classroom.

WANT TO BE A STAR CHALLENGER?

You and your class can have your own Challenger Center adventure—a mission to the Moonbase, a day aboard the space station, the launch of a space probe.

You and your team will:
- Conduct experiments using robotic arms and glove boxes
- Assemble the electronics of a space probe
- Run medical tests and biological experiments
- Manage communications at Mission Control

There are 50 Challenger Learning Centers across the United States, Canada, the United Kingdom, and South Korea. To find the Challenger Center closest to you, go to www.challenger.org for an interactive map. Even if you don't live near a Center, you can still participate in online adventures and interactive learning experiences.

The website also has discussion groups to connect young space enthusiasts from around the world, along with interesting links to other resources, information about space program, and interactive games.

Challenger®
C E N T E R

www.Challenger.org

Catalyst Game Labs is dedicated to producing high-quality games and fiction that mesh sophisticated game mechanics with dynamic universes—all presented in a form that allows beginning players and long-time veterans to easily jump into our games and fiction readers to enjoy our stories even if they don't know the games.

Catalyst Game Labs is an imprint of InMediaRes Productions, LLC, which specialized in electronic publishing of professional fiction. This allows Catalyst to meld printed gaming material and fiction with all the benefits of electronic interfaces and online communities, creating a whole-package experience for any type of player or reader.

Find Catalyst Game Labs online at www.catalystgamelabs.com

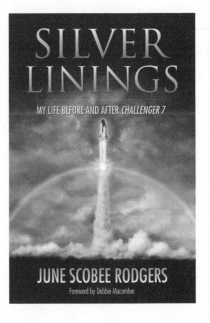

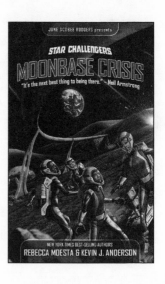